NUGGET CITY

WAYNE D. OVERHOLSER

SAGEBRUSH
Large Print Westerns

First published in Great Britain by Thorndike
First published in the United States by Five Star

Published in Large Print 2013 by ISIS Publishing Ltd.,
7 Centremead, Osney Mead, Oxford OX2 0ES
by arrangement with
The Golden West Literary Agency

CIP data is available for this title from the British Library

ISBN 978-0-7531-9136-1 (pb)

Printed and bound in Great Britain by
T. J. International Ltd., Padstow, Cornwall

CHAPTER
ONE

Ed McCoy stood in front of the Nugget City hotel, waiting for the stage, just as he had every week day afternoon since he had pinned on the sheriff's star more than a year ago, and as his father, Fist McCoy, had waited for the twenty-odd years he had been sheriff. Ed grinned as he thought about it. A habit now, he guessed, because today's Nugget City was nothing like the brawling mining camp it had been in the early days.

Ed didn't remember those days very well, although for some reason the memory of the stage wheeling in with a cloud of dust boiling up around it, the Jehu's yells, the crack of the whip, all combined to make a mental picture that remained clear in his mind. The coaches had been crowded with all kinds of people from the best to the worst. Fist had never paid much attention to the best, but he paid a lot of attention to the worst.

The stage was late today, and Ed started to turn toward his office in the courthouse, thinking there was no real reason for him to wait, when he saw the coach top the rise north of town. He watched as it approached, thinking it was probably empty as it was most of the time.

But today was different. Ed could hardly believe his eyes when a man stepped down from the coach and took the valise the driver handed to him. This was not the ordinary man who arrived in Nugget City to buy cattle or sell a line of merchandise or go fishing. His brand was plain to read. He wore two guns, carried butts forward, their cedar handles shiny with wear. Not many men in Marion County carried one gun, and certainly not two. It was equally certain they wouldn't be carried butt forward in the manner this fellow did.

The man turned toward the front door of the hotel, his eyes locking with Ed's for just a second, then he stepped up on the board walk and brushed past him without a nod or the slightest acknowledgment of his presence. The gunman wore a brown broadcloth suit and a black, broad-brimmed hat, a tall man, six feet two inches or more. He moved with an easy, cat-like grace. He would, Ed thought, be fast with his guns. Some men carried guns because they felt they were not properly dressed without them, and some wore them because the guns gave them an appearance of authority which they otherwise lacked, but there was no doubt in Ed's mind about this man. He wore them to use.

Stepping inside the hotel, Ed watched the gunman sign the register and take a key from the outstretched hand of Al Fleming, the hotel owner. He said to Fleming: "I don't know how long I'll be here," and, picking up his suitcase, climbed the stairs.

Fleming stood motionless, staring at the man until he disappeared up the stairs, then he asked: "What do you figure he's here for?"

Ed walked to the desk and spun the register. The man's name was John Brown, or so he had written. He had not recorded his place of residence. John Brown probably wasn't his real name. Chances were he was on the dodge.

"I asked you a question, damn it," Fleming said, a nervous edge to his voice.

Ed was startled because Al Fleming was usually a very calm man. "Why, hell, Al, how would I know why he's here?"

"Then you'd better find out," Fleming said, his voice raised to what was close to a scream. "That man's a killer."

"Maybe," Ed said. "Maybe not. The fact that he's carrying two guns doesn't make him a killer." He paused, noting the pallor that had come into the hotel man's face. "You know him?"

"Hell, no," Fleming said, his gaze not meeting Ed's.

This wasn't right, Ed thought. He had known Fleming from the day the man had come to Nugget City and bought the hotel more than ten years ago. He had always been a quiet, law-abiding citizen who had run a clean hotel and had gone out of his way to please his patrons. Now, for some reason, he was a badly frightened man.

"What's the matter with you, Al?" Ed asked. "He say something to scare you?"

"No." Fleming looked up, and then lowered his gaze again. "It ain't logical, Sheriff. What's he doing here? There's nothing to bring a man like him to Nugget City. I tell you he's up to no good."

Ed had the same feeling, a gut feeling that wasn't due to logic. Fleming was right about one thing. There wasn't anything in Marion County to bring a gunman here. At least he hoped there wasn't.

"I can't run a man out of the county just because he's packing two guns," Ed said.

"No, reckon not," Fleming agreed, "but I sure don't like it, him being in my hotel. Damn it, Ed, he even looks like the devil."

That, Ed thought, was pulling the bow a little long. A moment later Brown appeared at the head of the stairs. He came down slowly, one step at a time. Ed moved back from the desk, studying the man, and decided grimly that Brown did look a little bit the way he had always imagined the devil looked. He didn't have horns or a tail, but he did have a long, pointed nose, a sharp chin, and the blackest and coldest eyes Ed had ever seen.

The gunman stopped at the desk, pointed at some cigars under the glass counter, and took five out of the box when Fleming set it on the counter. He tossed a coin onto the glass top, slipped four into his coat pocket, and bit off the end of the fifth one. He walked to the door, spit the cigar end into the street, and struck a match. He held the flame to the end of the cigar, pulled on it, and blew out a great cloud of smoke, then

4

stepped through the door and sat down on one of the chairs on the hotel porch.

Fleming came out from behind his desk and moved to stand a step from Ed. He said in a hoarse whisper: "I tell you, you've got to get him out of town."

The thought occurred to Ed that Fleming did know the man, that he was afraid Brown would uncover something in his past that he didn't want the people of Nugget City to know. Fleming had always seemed like a colorless human being and not a man to have a past that was noteworthy in any respect.

"I'll talk to him," Ed said, and stepped through the door, taking a chair beside Brown's.

He lifted a can of Prince Albert from his pocket and filled his pipe, replaced the can, and tamped the tobacco into the bowl. He lighted it, puffed for a moment, then leaned back in his chair, glancing sideways at the gunman. Odd, he thought, how Brown pretended he didn't exist.

Ed took the pipe out of his mouth. "Where you from?"

Brown turned his head to stare at Ed. He said: "That, my friend, is none of your damned business."

The note of hostility was razor sharp. Ed said mildly: "Well, now, I ain't so sure about that. Right now this is a purty peaceful country. If you'll look at the mountain over yonder, you'll notice them mine dumps. We had a good mining business going at one time. A lot of people lived here, and a lot of money was being passed around. A man like you didn't mean much. Too many of you were around. Now the mining business is gone. We

5

depend on ranching. The way I see it, a man like you don't have no business in Marion County."

Brown tongued the cigar to the other side of his mouth and took a tight grip on it, his jaw muscles bulging like two little marbles. He said: "All that ain't nothing to me, one way or the other." He nodded at the badge on Ed's shirt. "Town marshal?"

"County sheriff," Ed answered. "There's a little more to it. We're sitting on what you might call a powder keg. We've got two big ranches in the valley. There's the M Bar at the upper end. Owned by a man named Curt Maulden. Then there's Rafter E at the lower end. Pete Egan owns that one. For reasons nobody seems right clear about, they hate each other like poison. Some day one of 'em will start shooting. When they do, there'll be hell to pay."

Brown shrugged, pulled on his cigar, and stared across the street at the red brick front of the Marion County Bank. "Still ain't no skin off my nose."

"Damn it, it may be off ours," Ed said hotly, "if either one of 'em hired you."

"Might be a job for me with one of 'em," Brown said, suddenly interested.

Ed shook his head. "It's been building over the years. I don't aim to let it blow up. If either of 'em hired you, you're leaving on the next stage."

Brown laughed. "They didn't, so you can settle down, but, if one of 'em had, you couldn't make that stick. I haven't broken no laws, unless sitting out here in front of the hotel is a crime in this two-bit town."

6

"Sometimes I go by the spirit of the law more than the letter," Ed said grimly. "I'd make it stick, all right. I've worked too hard to keep things peaceable to let a tough hand like you move in and start the ball. I've got one gunslick in the county now named Red Mike Kelso who works for Egan. I sure ain't letting a second get a toe-hold hereabouts."

"Red Mike Kelso," Brown repeated. "Never heard of him. I guess he don't amount to much."

"I don't know if he amounts to much or not," Ed said, "but he's a cocky bastard. If you're here very long, he'll jump you for some reason or another."

"Then he'll be a dead man," Brown said in a tone of certainty, his cold eyes fixed on Ed's face. "I came from Montana, if it is any business of yours. My name really is John Brown, and I ain't no relation to the *hombre* they strung up after the affair at Harper's Ferry."

Ed rose, thinking Brown was the most unfriendly man he had ever met. He hadn't done anything to interest the law, but his answers hadn't taken care of all the questions in Ed's mind, either. More than that, it was odd.

For just a moment Ed stood motionless, staring down at the gunman, then he turned away and walked the block to the courthouse. It was a fine, two-story building that had been erected in Marion County's glory days when everyone dreamed of Nugget City becoming another Cripple Creek or Leadville, and now the courthouse was a mocking reminder of those shattered dreams.

Ed walked through the long, dark hall to his office in the back of the building. The jail that opened into the office was empty, as it had been most of the time since Ed had taken the sheriff's star. The men he had locked up were cowboys on the prod who had disturbed the peace, or drunks who needed a place to sleep it off.

The past year had been pleasant enough, Ed thought, as he sat down at his desk, still puffing his pipe, too pleasant as a matter of fact. In that year he had not been tested. He was twenty-three, young enough for some in Marion County to wonder if he could handle an emergency. He knew very well that he had not been appointed to finish his father's term because of anything he had accomplished, but because he was Fist McCoy's son. He walked in his father's shadow, a father who was a legend, and now, leaning back in his chair, he wondered if he would ever be clear of that shadow.

This situation he was facing might very well be the testing he had known he would face some day. He opened a desk drawer and took out a pile of reward dodgers, his mind still on John Brown and what his coming to Nugget City might mean. Nothing, perhaps.

So far Curt Maulden and Pete Egan had kept the peace, but the situation was like a smoldering fire, no trouble until a breeze fanned it into a consuming flame. On Maulden's part the problem was the man's sheer cussedness. Ed was in love with his daughter, Judy, and Judy was in love with him, but marriage seemed out of the question as long as her father was alive, or until he changed his attitude, and that, Ed thought bitterly, was the last thing that would happen.

Maulden had told Ed to stay off the M Bar's range, or he'd shoot him. If Maulden loved anyone, it was Judy, but Ed questioned that. He seemed rather to hate everyone except Judy, a hatred that had been multiplied many times when he'd lost a leg a couple of years ago. He'd always been contrary, but it had grown into a sort of insanity. Of all the people he hated, Pete Egan received the bitterest focus, and Ed had to admit that Maulden had some reason to hate him, or at least fear him.

On the other hand, Egan was afraid of Maulden because the M Bar controlled the head waters of Nugget Creek, and Egan's spread depended on that water for its very existence. If Maulden ever decided to divert the flow of water, the Rafter E would no longer be a viable ranch. Maulden had threatened to do it more than once. Ed was sure that sooner or later, as vindictive as Maulden was, he would do it.

Ed finished going through the reward dodgers. It seemed that John Brown was not a wanted man. At least there apparently was no reward out for him. Ed shoved the stack of papers back, swearing softly. What was the man doing here?

CHAPTER
TWO

Cathy Allen sat in her living room near the window overlooking Main Street as she basted the hem of Mrs Thorn's dress. Mrs Thorn was the banker's wife, a very large woman who considered herself the social arbiter of Nugget City. She was, too, Cathy admitted, not because of her good looks or gracious manner, but simply because Sam Thorn held the future of nearly every Nugget City inhabitant in the palm of his hand.

Thorn had showed up in Nugget City more than ten years ago after the boom days were gone, bought the bank, and then gradually in one way or another managed to acquire most of the town property or held mortgages on the property he didn't own. As long as people had marched to his tune, everything went fine. For those who had jumped the track, the future was bleak. The next time a payment or rent was due, the unfortunate rebel was out of a home or place of business. The result was that folks marched to Mrs Thorn's tune as well as her husband's.

Cathy hated the woman with good reason. She was impossible to please, and she grew more unreasonable with time. The cause, Cathy suspected, was that Mrs Thorn became fatter each month. As she found it harder to get around, Cathy thought, she probably hated herself a little more for each added pound.

That situation, as far as Cathy was concerned, was going to change very soon. She kept one eye on the street as she sewed. The stage was due, and in spite of herself she became more nervous as the minutes passed. John Brown would be on it. She had not seen him since he had ridden out of Montana in a hurry after he'd shot a member of the posse that had been chasing him.

Cathy reminded herself that it had not been John's fault. He had been hired by some cattleman to drive the gangsters out of the country. The trouble was the cowmen were outnumbered at the polls, so the sheriff who had been elected in the last election was a sodbuster. The result was that the sheriff went after John on a trumped-up charge. In a running fight one of the posse members was shot and killed, and John headed for Canada and had been there ever since.

A moment later she was relieved to hear the stage. She rose and dropped the dress on her cutting table. Her front room had been her work room from the time she had come to Nugget City and put out her sign — **DRESSMAKING AND ALTERATIONS**. She had drifted south after John's hasty departure, looking for a place to start over, and more or less by accident had reached Nugget City. Finding the town had no dressmaker, she had settled down and had done well.

Standing in the doorway, she watched the stage pass. She saw the head of one passenger and, although she had only a glimpse, she was sure it was John. She found a scrap of paper and a pencil and hastily scribbled:

Log house third from corner in next block south.

She folded it several times until it was very small, dropped it into her pocket, and left the house.

The bank was her first stop. She paused at a table long enough to make out a withdrawal slip. She was taking out every cent she had in the bank, and almost laughed aloud when she thought of what Sam Thorn would say when he learned what she had done. He hated to see anyone take money out of the bank. She walked quickly to the teller's cage and presented the slip.

The cashier studied it for a moment then said, as if he couldn't believe she really meant it: "You want all of this in cash?"

Cathy nodded, wondering how else she could take it, and he whirled and disappeared into Thorn's private office. Thorn appeared a moment later, holding the slip in front of him as he stared at it while walking slowly toward the cashier's cage. He was a fat man, not as fat as his wife, but in Cathy's opinion he was even more obnoxious than his wife. She at least was exactly what she appeared to be, but he was the worst hypocrite Cathy could recall having met.

"You aren't leaving town, are you, Cathy?" he said, his tone forbidding her to do any such thing.

He was smiling sweetly which belied his tone of voice. He always used that smile when he was talking

12

about anything that he found unpleasant, and taking money out of his bank was very unpleasant.

"Yes," she said sharply, hoping he'd get the point that it was none of his business.

He still stood, staring at the withdrawal slip, hesitating as if hoping she'd change her mind. Finally he said: "We can't let you do that. Myra never found anyone who could make a satisfactory dress for her until you came to town. Her size, of course, makes her a difficult subject."

Cathy wished Mrs Thorn had told her just once that her work was satisfactory, but she had never heard anything but complaints from the woman. She said: "Sorry, Mister Thorn, but I have to go. I just want my money. It is mine, you know."

He sighed, opened a drawer, and began counting out the bills. He said, when he finished: "If you change your mind, we'll be pleased to have your business again."

She took the money, folded it, and dropped it into her pocket, thinking he would indeed love to have her money back in his safe. She whirled and stalked out, her skirt flying away from her trim ankles. She was aware that she was the most attractive woman in town and that every man, single or married, was aware of her face and was aroused by it. She smiled as she walked to the street door, her hips swaying seductively. She knew that both Thorn and the cashier would watch her as long as she was in sight.

She was surprised that Thorn had not propositioned her as he had the school teacher, Sally York, but perhaps he sensed what her answer would be. She felt her skin crawl, feeling unclean just from her brief encounter with the man. He was despicable, she told herself, and, wondering if she should consider him oily or slimy, she decided that slimy was the proper adjective.

She glanced toward the hotel, her heart pounding. It had been so long since she had seen John. She looked away quickly and a moment later stepped into the Mercantile, hoping that she wasn't breathing hard or that her face wasn't too rosy from the warmth that swept through her. She had wondered so many times in the last six weeks since she'd received his letter if he would actually get here. But there he was, sitting in front of the hotel and looking exactly as she remembered him.

She was surprised to see a number of women inside the store, including Mrs Thorn. They were lined up in front of the windows, staring at John Brown. Cathy moved past them to the meat counter, not particularly wanting to hear what they were saying, but unable to keep the words from beating at her ears.

"Why doesn't that cowardly Ed McCoy run him out of town?" Mrs Thorn demanded in a little-girl voice that was incongruous, coming from such a huge woman. "The man's a killer. None of us will be safe as long as he's in town."

No one ever argued with Mrs Thorn, but Buck Moore, the store owner, said mildly: "Gunmen don't kill women, Missus Thorn."

"This one will," Mrs Thorn said, her tone rebuking Moore. "You mark my word."

14

"Well," said Mrs Luke Jones, the preacher's wife, "I'm not going to feel safe as long as he's in town."

"I don't know why he'd come here," said Mrs Cotter, the doctor's wife, plaintively. "We have been getting along so well."

"He wouldn't come unless he had a reason," Sally York said in a worried tone.

Sally was standing beside Mrs Thorn. They made a strange contrast, Cathy thought, with Mrs Thorn as big as a house and Sally as slim as a fence post. Cathy wondered why Sally would be concerned about John's presence unless she had something to hide and was afraid he would expose her.

Cathy wondered, too, if Mrs Thorn suspected what went on between her husband and Sally. Maybe she did and simply chose to accept it, so she could continue to have the advantages of a banker's wife. That would be like her, Cathy reflected. Pride would not be as important to her as the luxury and social prestige she now enjoyed.

Buck Moore finally noticed Cathy and hurried to her. "Sorry," he said. "I didn't see you over here."

"You were too busy talking about the stranger to see any customers," Cathy said sharply.

He nodded. "Yeah, they're all scared. I thought I could reassure them, but I couldn't. They've got no cause to worry. Maybe some men in town have, but not the women."

"Of course not," she agreed. "Have you got any fresh meat, Buck?"

"I sure do," he said promptly. "I just butchered two days ago. A fine young Rafter E steer I bought from Pete Egan."

"Can you cut me two steaks?" she asked.

"Of course," he said. "It will just take a minute."

He hurried through the back door. Probably, she thought, he had butchered two weeks ago instead of two days, but it didn't make any difference. He had an ice house back of the store, and his meat was never spoiled. She stood listening to the talk of the coming disaster, of blame piled high on the sheriff's head, of how old Fist McCoy would have had the man on his way before this, and on and on.

Moore returned with the meat, and she paid for it. She walked out of the store, bitterness a poison in her. Even in an old mining camp like Nugget City, snobbery was as evident as Cathy had found it in bigger towns. Every other woman in town, even Sally York, who taught during the day and whored at night, had been accepted socially, but not Cathy Allen.

She had never been sure why, unless the other women were afraid she would steal their husbands. They needn't worry, she thought. The only man in town she'd look at twice was Ed McCoy, and he couldn't see anybody but Judy Maulden. It didn't make a hell of a lot of difference, she told herself as she crossed the street. She'd soon be gone, but Sally York would be here, teaching Nugget City's children and making Sam Thorn happy.

She purposely stumbled as she passed John, flipping the note to him, hoping that her stumble wouldn't attract the eyes of the women in the store. She was careful not to glance at him as she regained her balance and hurried on toward her house, but out of the corner of her eye she caught his quick motion as he caught the ball of paper.

While she walked toward her house, the resentment and bitterness and hatred that had grown in her through the months she had lived in Nugget City boiled over. She reached her house, banged the door behind her, and stomped across the front room into her kitchen where she slammed her meat down on the table. It was so like those damned women to condemn John before he had done anything to be condemned for, to fear him and even think he had come here to make war on them. She fled into her bedroom, threw herself on the bed, and began to cry. She cried for only a minute before her mind turned to her plan, the plan that had brought John here, the plan that would get even with Thorn and his monstrous wife, and Sally York, the hypocrites who had the gall to look down on her.

She lay on her back, wishing that the time would pass quickly. She felt the physical need of a man, a need that had not been satisfied in the year since John had left Montana on the run. Tomorrow, or the day after, she would go to Sam Thorn, and then she and John would be on their way out of Nugget City as fast as they could split the breeze.

CHAPTER
THREE

The first thing Ed's mother asked when he came home for supper was: "Who is that man sitting in front of the hotel?"

Ed hung his hat on a nail near the back door, pumped water into a basin, and washed and dried before he answered, then, as he ran a comb through his hair, he said: "Says his name is John Brown."

"Where did he come from?" she asked as she dished up the food.

Ed sat down at the table, thinking that by now probably everybody knew about John Brown, and likely all of them were thinking the same thing that Al Fleming was, that Ed ought to run the man out of town.

"He didn't give a home address when he registered," Ed answered, "but he told me he came from Montana. He didn't say what town."

"You think he was lying?" his mother asked.

"Probably," Ed said, as he helped himself to the mashed potatoes. "If he wasn't, he didn't tell me anything. Montana's a big state."

"Well," Mrs McCoy said angrily, "you'd think he owns the whole town, sitting there on the hotel porch just looking us over. He's scared everybody to death. It ain't natural, Ed."

He grinned as he cut his steak. "No, it ain't, but then he's got a perfect right to sit on the front porch of the hotel if he wants to. He hasn't done anything to give me the right to question him, but I did ask a few questions because Al Fleming was so worked up about him being there."

"It's an old story," she said heavily. "I used to hear it from your pa over and over. You can't arrest a man until he's committed a crime. I'd say it was plain that he was sent for by somebody to kill somebody. A gunman like him don't ride around the country just for the ride."

Ed went on eating, not saying anything. His mother was dead right, which didn't change a damned thing. If Brown had been brought here by anyone, it would be either Pete Egan or Curt Maulden. The part he couldn't figure was why Al Fleming was so jumpy. Then he remembered what his mother had just said.

"What do you mean by saying he's scaring everybody to death?" Ed asked.

"I guess I didn't mean everybody," she answered. "Just a bunch of women who were in the store this afternoon. Missus Thorn. Missus Rayburn. Sally York. Several others."

"Why were they scared?"

"I dunno." She shrugged. "Buck kept telling them a gunman wouldn't come here to kill women. Maybe they were worrying about their men folks. I know I was worrying about you."

"You always worried about Pa when somebody like Brown turned up," Ed said.

"And now I've got to do it all over again for you," Mrs McCoy said. "Why you ever pinned that star on in the first place is a mystery to me. You could have had a good job with Pete Egan."

"For thirty a month and beans," Ed said hotly, "and have Curt Maulden hating me more than he does now. We've gone over this enough, Ma."

"I know," she said wearily. "I guess you're old enough to make up your mind, although goodness knows I never saw the day when you didn't do just what you pleased."

"I got that from you," Ed said, grinning. "Pa always told me that."

"It ain't true," Mrs McCoy snapped. "He said it just to plague me."

Ed reached for the meat platter, frowning. "Something's been chewing on me, now that you've told me about Brown scaring everybody while all he's done is to sit in a chair. I got to thinking that most of the folks who live here have been in Nugget City for years. I guess Cathy Allen is the only newcomer we've got."

His mother nodded. "I don't see what that's got to do with anything."

"Maybe nothing," he admitted, "but folks drift into boom towns when they want to get lost in a crowd, maybe folks who are wanted by the law back where they came from, or maybe they're trying to hide from somebody who's after them. Take Al Fleming. Talk about being scared to death. He acted like he thought Brown was after him. It might be the same with the women. Or their husbands."

Mrs McCoy nodded. "It seemed to me they were making more scare talk than the occasion called for."

"Probably cussing me out, too," Ed said.

"I'm afraid they were," she agreed, "but they didn't seem to worry about me hearing what they said. I didn't defend you because you told me not to. Missus Thorn was the worst."

"That bitch," he said. "She probably wishes Pa was wearing the star."

"That's what she said," Mrs McCoy replied, "but, when your pa was alive, she had plenty to say bad about him. I guess I wasn't very polite, but I finally did tell her what I thought of her. She's the meanest woman I ever saw."

Ed rose, too jumpy to sit here, or even take his usual walk around town after supper. His mother asked uneasily: "What are you going to do?"

Sometimes he thought she still considered him a boy. Well, damn it, he'd grown up into a man six feet two who weighed over two hundred pounds of good, hard muscle. If he couldn't take care of himself now, when could he?

"I'm going to take a ride," he said shortly as he turned toward the back door.

"Where to?" she pressed.

He put a hand on the knob and looked back at her, suddenly remembering this was the way she had been with his father. She was a small woman in her early sixties, gray haired and wrinkled, too wrinkled for her age. She had worked hard from the day she'd been married, first on a ranch in Texas, then in New Mexico, and finally here in Colorado when Fist had decided to turn miner. That hadn't lasted long. He became a lawman, first town marshal and then county sheriff. Those had been dangerous days with Nugget City not at all like the sleepy, half-deserted town it was now.

He had no right to be angry with her, he thought, and was ashamed. "Just out of town a piece," he said. "Quit worrying, Ma. You had your time of worrying when Pa was alive."

"I know," she said as she walked to him. "It's foolish of me, but that man sitting in front of the hotel . . . I suppose he's still sitting there . . . just simply scared me out of my shoes. He doesn't belong here, Ed. It's like suddenly we're back in the old days when your pa was keeping the lid on a wild camp."

"He's only one man," Ed said. "Pa used to have to watch a dozen like him."

"There's other things, too," she said. "I'm afraid this man fits into them."

"Like what?" he asked.

"Well, the feud between Pete Egan and Curt Maulden for one," she answered. "They used to just quarrel, but now they're not doing anything. It's like a quiet spell before a storm." She turned, wiped her eyes, then went on. "I'm a foolish old woman, but I've got a bad feeling about them two."

"No use to borrow trouble before it gets here," he said.

"I know," she said, "but that's not all. It breaks my heart that you and Judy can't get married. It's time you were starting your own family. If Curt Maulden wasn't such a mean, stubborn old goat . . ."

"Judy's about ready to leave home," he said. "Curt's as crazy as a horse that's been in a patch of loco weed. Now he's getting worse. She won't put up with him much longer." He opened the door and stepped onto the back porch. "I'll be back in a little while."

He strode across the back yard to the barn where he kept his roan gelding. He wished that what he'd said about Judy's leaving her father was true, but it wasn't. He'd said it just to make his mother feel better. It was true that Maulden was getting worse, and Ed worried about Judy's safety. Maulden hadn't laid a hand on her for years, but a man as crazy as he was could do anything if he was upset or defied. All it would take for Maulden to go berserk would be for Judy to tell him she was leaving home to marry Ed McCoy. She would tell him if she decided to leave. She had talked to Ed about it many times, and he had tried to tell her she should simply ride away some day and not go back, but she always said she couldn't do that.

Ed finished saddling his roan and was leading him out of the barn just as Sam Thorn walked around the house. When he saw Ed, he yelled: "Hold on, McCoy. I want to talk to you."

Ed swung into the saddle, but remained where he was until Thorn reached him. He swore under his breath. The banker was the last man he wanted to see.

"I'm here about that gunslick who came in on the stage today," Thorn said, puffing because he had crossed the back yard in what was a sort of plodding run. "I want him out of town."

"Why?" Ed asked. "He hasn't committed any crime."

"Because he will, damn it," Thorn snapped. "A man of his caliber doesn't come to a town like Nugget City just to pass the time of day. You know that. He's dangerous. I'm telling you to get him on the stage in the morning. It leaves at eight, you know."

Ed shook his head. "I've looked through my reward dodgers. As far as I know, he's not a wanted man. The law has no right to make him leave town, but I assure you that if he does break a law . . ."

Thorn reached up and grabbed Ed's arm that was nearest to him and shook it in a wild frenzy. "McCoy, I didn't come here to argue with you or to discuss the weaknesses of our legal system. I'm ordering you to get that man out of town or, by God, I'll have your star."

Ed jerked his arm free, a red haze dancing before his eyes. It was all he could do to keep from stepping out of the saddle and hammering his fist into the man's protruding belly. Thorn would not have taken this attitude with Fist McCoy, and Ed had no intention of letting the banker take it with him.

"You've been pretty high and mighty for quite a while, Sam," Ed said, "using your bank to put a strangle hold on everybody in town. My house happens to be one that is free of your mortgages, so don't threaten me if I don't jump when you whistle." He took

24

a long breath and added: "You run the bank, and I'll run the sheriff's office."

Thorn's face turned red. He started to say something, choked and sputtered, and finally managed: "I'm going to see the county commissioners tomorrow. I'll see they take your star away from you!"

"You do that, Sam," Ed said and, touching his roan with his spurs, rode down the alley to the street.

CHAPTER
FOUR

For a full minute Sam Thorn stood, shaking his fist in the direction Ed McCoy had gone and shouting curses after him, then he realized the futility of what he was doing and wheeled back toward the street. He walked the two blocks to his house very slowly. He was tired. What was worse — he was humiliated. It was the first time the young sheriff had openly defied him, and he was not used to defiance.

When he reached the house, he found his wife sprawled out on the leather couch, an unmoving mass of flesh. This was her usual position when he came home for supper. Neither of them spoke as he walked past her into his bedroom and hung his coat and hat in his closet, then he returned to the living room and sat down in a Morris chair.

His wife stared at him a moment, as if gauging his mood, then she said: "What have you done about that horrible killer who has been sitting in front of the hotel all afternoon?"

"Nothing," he said.

"Nothing!" She sat up, shocked. "You're going to do nothing to get rid of a man who is threatening our lives?"

"Oh, hell," he said disgustedly. "He's not threatening your life. Mine, maybe, but not yours. You'd be a lot happier if you'd stay home and do a little work instead of wagging your tongue in the store and scaring everybody to death as well as yourself."

"*Humpf*," she said. "Us women can be scared, too, you know."

He was silent. Over the years he had learned that arguing with Myra was the most useless activity in which he could engage. He stared at her, thinking how repulsive she was, and he wondered as he had so many times why he had married her. She was of no use to him in any way. In fact, she was a liability because of her gossiping and her way of lording it over the other women of the town.

Nancy Jones, the preacher's daughter, appeared in the dining room doorway and announced that supper was ready. Nancy was the Thorns' housekeeper, cook, maid, and everything else that Mrs Thorn needed. She was an excellent cook, but she seldom satisfied her employer, and Sam Thorn often wondered how she could force herself to stay.

It was, of course, a matter of economics. The preacher had a large family, and Nancy's meager earnings made the difference between a living and actual privation. Thorn was never a generous man, but he was practical and, when he thought of the meals Mrs Thorn had prepared before he hired Nancy, he decided that a little generosity was just common sense, so he gave Nancy a sizable bonus at Christmas and another on her birthday.

Thorn rose and followed his wife into the dining room. They sat down, and Nancy served. Mrs Thorn immediately began complaining — first, the roast was too well done, then, the gravy was too thick — and suddenly Sam had had enough.

He slammed a beefy hand against the table and shouted: "My God, Myra, what does it take to satisfy you?" He turned to Nancy who was standing in the kitchen doorway, a shocked expression on her face. "It's a fine meal, Nancy. Try not to pay any attention to her."

For a moment Myra Thorn stared at her husband as Nancy fled into the kitchen. "Well," she said, "you are in a fine mood tonight. Maybe that gunman has you scared, too."

He had indeed, Thorn thought, but he would never admit that to his wife. He ate rapidly, wanting to get out of the house as soon as he could. Until this moment he had never fully realized how much he hated his wife. At various times he had thought how wonderful it would be, if he could get rid of her and marry Sally York, but, since his wife seemed to be in good health, she would probably live for years. The solution was to kill her, and now, listening to her eat, he thought it would be no worse than justifiable homicide. He might as well have married a hog. Maybe, he thought darkly, killing her wouldn't be any greater crime than slaughtering a fat sow.

He rose, walked into the bedroom, put on his coat and hat, and left the house. He seldom stayed home for a full evening, and he never risked going to Sally's place until it was completely dark.

Unlocking the street door of the bank, he went in and shut the door behind him, then crossed the lobby to his office. He sat down at his desk, lit a cigar, and leaned back in his swivel chair. He began to explore various methods of killing his wife. Smothering her with a pillow was probably the best, and he could blame it on a heart attack.

Old Doc Cotter would agree, but, even if the doctor had his doubts, he would not express them to anyone. The trouble was — and he knew this very well — he was not a killer. He would never go through with it. The few pleasant hours he spent with Sally each evening helped him bear the tensions he felt when he was with Myra. It was a relationship he could not give up, but he also knew it could not go on forever. He was caught, he told himself bitterly, caught in a trap from which there was no escape.

Then, for the first time since he had left Ed McCoy, he turned his thoughts to the gunman who had come, uninvited, to Nugget City, and the threat the man might be to his way of life. A flood of memories he had kept dammed up in his consciousness for years now began returning, of the holdup in the little Missouri town where he had started working when he was eighteen.

He had worked in that bank for twelve years, mentally threatening every day to quit but never doing it because jobs were hard to get — that is, jobs he liked. He abhorred the thought of doing any kind of manual labor. Besides, he kept hoping the owner, an old man who enjoyed poor health, would raise his pay or make him a partner.

He'd found a girl he wanted to marry, a girl who would have made a far better wife than Myra, but there was no way he could have supported her on his small salary. He had considered various ways of robbing the bank, but no practical method had occurred to him until the morning when a masked man walked in and ordered Thorn to fill the flour sack he was carrying with money from the safe. A cocked .45 lined on Thorn's chest was a convincing argument.

After that several things happened very fast. The owner, hearing the commotion, came charging out of his office, firing a revolver the instant he cleared the door. He missed, but the robber shot and killed him. For a second the man's attention was diverted, a second that gave Thorn time to grab the revolver that was kept in the safe for this very purpose. He whirled and gunned down the outlaw before he could shoot Thorn.

He never knew for sure how he got the idea of taking the money. Maybe it was just that the possibility had been in his mind so long that he recognized the opportunity and acted upon it without conscious thought. He picked up the sack with the money he had dropped into it and ran into the owner's office. He yanked a desk drawer open, shoved the sack into it, and ran out of the office in time to kneel beside his dead employer. That was where the sheriff found him when he arrived a moment later.

Thorn was considered a hero. Of course, no one had any idea how much money was in the safe, so the thought never occurred to anyone that there could be more than was found in the safe when the sheriff arrived. Thorn said that the robber had ordered him to fill the bank's canvas bags with money, and he had started to do that when the banker began shooting.

Everyone trusted Sam Thorn. The banker's wife asked him to stay on to manage the bank once it reopened and until a new manager was appointed. She then ordered it closed until after the funeral, telling Thorn to count the money that was in the safe and list the bank's assets and obligations.

Thorn worked hard that first night, remaining in the bank until after dark. When he left, the flour sack with the money was under his coat. He left through the back door and followed the alley to the little house he was renting. He was sure that no one would be suspicious of him or search his house, but as a precaution he placed the money in several glass jars and buried them in the flour bin in his pantry.

After that it was a matter of waiting and looking for an excuse to quit. That happened about a month after the robbery, when the widow hired a cousin to run the bank. Thorn pretended to be indignant that he was passed over, saying that he felt he deserved the job and he had no intention of working under another man. He felt that his years of loyal service were being unrewarded, so he resigned in a huff and left town on the train the following day.

He drifted after that for a time, finally deciding to try the mining country, hoping to find an opportunity to start a bank of his own. Nugget City, having no bank after the mines played out, gave him the opportunity he sought. He realized business would be slow, but there was a chance the mines would come back if the price of silver went up. Besides, there was enough ranching to keep the town going. Too, with property prices at rock bottom, he saw the opportunity for some shrewd investments.

The year after he opened the bank, he married Myra. Now, sitting here at his desk, he told himself that was the biggest mistake he had ever made. She had been slender then, and rather pretty, and she had some money which they used to buy the house where they lived, a fine, two-story brick structure with a mansard roof and an iron fence around the yard.

The house had been built by the owner of the best producing mine in Marion County and, when the mine played out, he moved away and locked up the house. Thorn bought it for a fraction of its cost, and Myra never let him forget that it was her money they had used to buy the house.

He was sure that no one suspected how he had gotten his own money. Still, the possibility had been in the back of his mind that someone might be curious and trace his career to his first job. Or someone back there might have guessed what had happened and had started looking for him. When the cousin had taken the bank over, he had expressed surprise that there was so little cash in the safe. Suppose he had hired this gunman to find Sam Thorn?

He shook his head, telling himself that after all this time he had no reason to worry. He had kept his name because he'd been afraid he might run into someone who knew him and would naturally be suspicious about any name change. But now, he told himself, that had been a mistake, and the possibility that the gunman had traced him to Nugget City was so frightening that he could not put it out of his thoughts even though his conscious mind told him it was stupid to worry about it at this late date.

Then his mind turned to his affair with Sally York. Losing her, he told himself glumly, was a bigger threat than the chance of his past thievery being exposed. Suddenly he rose, swearing at himself for being scared when there was no reason for it. If he only knew why that damned gunman had showed up, he could quit worrying.

He noticed that the darkness was complete, so there was no reason to dally here any longer. Usually he stopped in the Belle Union to have a drink, but tonight he needed Sally, needed the softness of her body, her passion, and most of all the love she had for him. Love was an experience he had never felt before he'd met Sally, and only then did he realize how empty his life had been.

He left the bank, his thoughts centered on Sally, and he hurried his steps, the desire for her a frenzied need in his loins.

CHAPTER
FIVE

Cathy did not expect to see John Brown until after dark. Not that there was any necessity to keep their relationship a secret. It was just that the knowledge might detract from the image her neighbors had of John, if they knew she was responsible for his being here, and that was an image she particularly wanted Sam Thorn to have. She had mentioned that in one of her letters, but John had been on the move so much she wasn't sure if he received all of them. Obviously he had received at least the one in which she had given him instructions about staying away until dark, or he would have been here before now.

She started preparing supper while it was still daylight. By the time it was fully dark, she had the meal ready except for the meat, which wouldn't take long to fry. She filled the fire box of her range with wood, then turned to a window to stare into the darkness. Impatience rose in her but only for a moment before she heard the back door open.

She whirled just as John Brown shut the door. He stood there, grinning at her, then she was in his arms, holding him, and crying, and saying over and over: "You're here, John. You're really here."

He pushed her back and, putting a hand under her chin, tipped her face up and stared down at her. "Of course, I'm here. I told you I'd come."

He kissed her, and she clung to him, her lips refusing to be satisfied. Presently he pushed her back a second time, saying: "I'm hungry. You gonna fix that?"

"Of course I am," she said. "I'm sorry. I'm just so damned glad to see you." She set the frying pan on the front of the stove and dropped the steaks into it. "It won't take long."

He came up behind her and put his arms around her. "We could go to bed first," he said.

She giggled. "There's time enough for that later. We've got something to do first, but it'll wait until after we eat. Now get away from me so I can work. There's hot water in the tea kettle. You can wash up while I'm finishing supper."

He picked up the kettle and poured the steaming water into a wash basin that was on a small table set against a wall. He dipped water from a nearby bucket to cool the water that was in the basin, washed his face and hands, combed his hair, then threw the water out through the back door. He walked to the table, pulled a chair back, and sat down.

"What was that herd of women doing in the store, staring at us through the windows?" he asked. "After you walked by, they came out of the store and stood on the walk, staring and cackling like a bunch of old hens."

"That's just what they are," she said angrily. "They were doing what I wanted them to do, only a lot more so. I hate 'em. I can't get out of this town fast enough."

She turned the steaks, then faced him. "You won't believe what I'm going to tell you, but they're afraid of you. They think you're going to kill them and everybody else in town, too, I guess."

He laughed. "Maybe I'd better rub somebody out so they'll be satisfied." Then he sobered. "They didn't really think I'd kill any of them, did they?"

"I dunno," she answered. "They were talking crazy. Almost hysterical. That fat woman is the banker's wife, and she's the worst of the bunch. I don't think there would have been much of that wild talk if it hadn't been for her." She was silent until she finished setting the food down on the table and took a chair across from Brown, then she said: "I knew you'd turn the town upside down just by sitting in front of the hotel like you've done. Not many strange men show up in Nugget City, least of all handsome ones who carry two guns. I wanted that to happen, but I didn't expect the women to go on like they have."

He ate ravenously, not taking time to talk until he had blunted the edge of his appetite, then he said: "You always were a tricky one, but I don't savvy this business of just sitting in front of the hotel and letting people see me. You said in your letter you had a scheme. I know it'll be crazy, but it had better be smart, too, bringing me to a place like this. I don't believe there's any money in this two-bit burg."

"There's money in the bank," Cathy said, "and we're going to get some of it."

"I ain't getting into no bank robbery," he snapped.

36

"That's not it," she said. "I'll tell you about it later. I knew people would talk about you and get scared, just having you in town. I may be able to do this job by myself, but you're my back-up, and I'll use you if I need you."

She rose and brought a lemon pie from the pantry and, cutting it into generous pieces, lifted two slices from the pan into two small side dishes and placed one in front of Brown, then brought the coffee pot from the stove and filled his cup.

When she sat down, he demanded: "When are you gonna tell me about this fancy scheme of yours?"

"Later," she said. "First I want to show you something."

"How much will it pay us?"

"I'm not sure," she answered, "but I'm going after ten thousand dollars, and I'll settle for half." She sipped her coffee, then set the cup down, and said vehemently: "John, I'm so damned tired of working my fingers off for women who don't appreciate my work and then try to whittle down what they pay me that I would be willing to rob a bank if I had to. I want a place of our own. I want children and a dog and chickens for me to take care of, and a herd of cattle for you."

He nodded. "Five thousand would do for a start, if we could find a spread far enough away so the law wouldn't be on my tail. I'm tired of looking over my shoulder to see if there's a dust cloud being kicked up by a posse." He paused, frowning, then asked: "What's this boy wonder of a sheriff like?"

"Ed McCoy? He's a good man. His problem is that he's trying to get out from under his daddy's shadow. Old Fist McCoy tamed Nugget City when it was a hell hole, or so I've heard. He ramrodded it until he died, then Ed was appointed, but he's never had much to do. Why? Did he make you any trouble?"

"No, but he asked a lot of questions which wasn't none of his business, and all the time I hadn't done anything except keep the seat of my pants warm. I may curry him down a little before I leave town."

"No," she snapped. "Don't you do nothing except sit in front of the hotel. Not unless I have trouble, and I'll sure tell you if I do." She rose. "Now we're taking a little walk to do some spying, then we'll go to bed, but right now you've got to be patient which is something you're not very good at."

"Oh, I dunno about that." He patted his stomach as he rose. "I'll say one thing for you. You ain't forgot how to cook. I hope you ain't forgot your other talents."

"I'll remember when it's time." She took his hand and led toward the back door. "It's not far, but we may have to wait. Maybe this isn't necessary, but I want you to see what I've been seeing, and what gave me my idea."

The darkness was complete except for the starshine from a clear sky, and that wasn't enough to keep them from stumbling as they made their way down the alley to a house at the other end of the block. They sat down behind some lilac bushes that lined the back side of the lot and waited.

"Don't look to me like anybody's in that house," Brown said after a few minutes had passed.

"Whisper," she breathed. "He'll be coming out pretty soon, and I don't want him to know we're here. I aim to surprise him in the morning."

"This sure is like you," he whispered. "Hell, it'd be easier to rob his bank and be done with it."

"And have the law after you again," she whispered back. "My way is a lot safer." A moment later the back door opened, and she added: "Here he comes."

For just a moment the door remained open, the lamp-light showing a big man and a slender woman in a tight embrace, then the man wheeled and left the house, and the door closed. Cathy squeezed Brown's hand as the man walked swiftly across the yard and, reaching the alley, turned to stride away in the opposite direction. He passed within ten feet of where they crouched behind the lilac bushes.

For several seconds they remained silent and motionless, then Cathy whispered: "We can go now."

"This ain't a man's way of doing things," he snorted. "I don't want nothing to do with your damned scheming."

They returned to Cathy's house, Brown muttering under his breath about her tricks. Cathy said angrily: "I've worked on this too long, and you've come too far just to kick it away."

They went back into the house through the back door. Cathy said: "Sit down. I'll get you a drink, then I'll tell you what I'm going to do."

"The sheriff was talking about a range war breaking out in the county," Brown said. "That's my kind of game. I could catch on with one side or the other."

She brought a bottle of whiskey and a glass from the pantry and poured a stiff drink, then she explained: "My God, John, can't you play my game for once? I've waited for you for a long time, and all you've produced for me is a bushel of worry."

He stared at her blankly for a moment, as if he hadn't thought of that, then he said: "Hell, I reckon you're right." He shrugged his shoulders. "All right, what is this fine scheme you're so worked up about?"

"The man you saw leaving the house was Sam Thorn," she answered. "He owns the bank and just about everything else in town. He's pious as hell. Elder in the church. Chairman of the school board. Talks a lot about what's good for the kids, but he manages to squelch any plan that would cost tax money no matter how good it is for the kids."

"Don't folks figure out the kind of gent he is?"

She shrugged. "Some do, but they likewise know his heart is a chunk of solid stone. He collects his rent and kicks anybody out of a house he owns if the rent's late. He'll take over a piece of property when a mortgage payment is due and isn't paid. People call that good business. What they don't know is that he sleeps with Sally York, the school teacher.

"She's so prim and sweet that sugar won't melt in her mouth. I hate the bitch. She thinks she's better'n I am. I'm just a dressmaker."

Brown laughed softly. "That's what's eating on you, ain't it?"

"That's sure part of it," she admitted.

"What makes you think nobody else in town knows what's going on?" he asked.

"I don't know I'm the only one," she said. "The difference is that, if anybody else knows, they're afraid to say anything. I'm not. I'll have it all over town if it comes to that."

"How'd you find out?"

"I'd been walking a lot at night when the weather wasn't too bad," she answered. "I can't sleep lots of times. Just wanting you, I guess, and thinking there wasn't any future for us. I figured you'd get strung up, if they ever caught you, or they'd send you to the pen for life. When I couldn't sleep, I'd get up and walk. Well, I saw Thorn in the alley several times headed toward his house, so I figured a woman had to be involved.

"Thorn sure hadn't been in the bank working that late, or drinking in the saloon. The only single woman in the block who didn't have a man was Sally York, so I began watching her house. Sure enough, old fat Sam left there every night along about midnight."

"His wife must know," Brown said thoughtfully. "I don't see how you can put enough pressure on him to do the job."

"It's the threat of public knowledge that will put the pressure on him," she said. "Maybe his wife does know and doesn't care. She'd probably rather have Sally taking over her wifely duties than do them herself." She paused, frowning. "One thing, though. Usually he opens the back door and slips out, keeping the room behind him dark so he can't be seen, but tonight they didn't even try to hide." Then she shrugged. "I don't know what that means. Maybe nothing."

"You say he's on the school board?"

Cathy nodded. "Chairman. Has been for years. I hear Sally's not much of a teacher, and some parents want her fired, but Thorn won't stand for it."

Brown sat back in his chair, one hand stroking his chin. "I can't believe this scheme is good enough to separate that old jasper from five thousand dollars."

"Oh, it will be," she said happily. "I know him. In the morning I'll go to the bank and tell him what I know. It'll be worth five thousand dollars to him to keep my mouth shut. What you can't savvy is that he takes so much pride in being a righteous man in the eyes of the community. Hardhearted, but righteous." She rose and took his hand. "Let's go to bed. I've waited long enough."

He rose with alacrity and followed her into the bedroom.

CHAPTER
SIX

Ed McCoy's roan gelding had not been ridden for a few days, and he was anxious to run, so Ed let him go for a short distance and then reined him down to a slower pace. He wanted to think. He could make no sense out of what was happening and that bothered him. Why had John Brown come to Nugget City in the first place, and why had his presence upset so many people?

Ed had intended to ride out to the Rafter E and talk to Pete Egan. Brown's appearance made some sense, if either Egan or Curt Maulden had sent for him, although if that was the case, why hadn't he rented a horse from the livery stable and ridden on to the ranch that had hired him?

After Ed had followed the creek for a mile or more, he decided that talking to Egan could wait until morning. He didn't really expect anything to happen tonight, but he was uneasy, and he knew he'd feel better if he stayed in town, so he turned his horse and rode back to Nugget City.

He left his horse in his barn and began his nightly cruise, going up one street and then turning at the edge of town and reversing his course on the next street. Fist

McCoy had always made these nightly rounds, and Ed had followed the same procedure from habit more than any sense of duty.

Ed had seldom, if ever, found anything out of the way or even interesting, but tonight he did. He had finished all but the last block of his route which was taking him down the alley on one side of Main Street when he approached the back of the hotel and saw a man slip out of the door at the top of the outside stairway and descend to the ground.

Al Fleming always kept a lighted lantern hanging above the door and another one above the door of the privy which was on a vacant lot across the alley. Ed did not recognize the man in the thin light until he reached the bottom of the stairway, and then he saw that it was John Brown who was leaving the hotel.

Ed stopped, surprised by this development. If Brown was indeed a stranger to everyone in town, why was he leaving the hotel? The gunman started down the alley at a brisk pace. Ed followed, keeping some distance between them.

A short time later, when they were in the next block, Brown turned off the alley and into the back yard of Cathy Allen's house. Ed hurried to get a clear view of what happened next, but he saw nothing except the quick opening of Cathy's back door, Brown's slipping into the house, and the door closing behind him.

Ed stood there several minutes, tempted to move on to the house and look through a window to see what was going on inside. He decided against it. Cathy would have the blinds pulled down. Besides, the idea of spying on a young woman by looking through her window went against his grain.

He strode on down the alley to the end of the block and turned toward Main Street. Maybe Cathy had sent for Brown, but why? He didn't know the girl well, but his mother had always been pleased by her work. As far as he knew, Cathy was the least likely person in town to call in a gunman.

He stepped into the lobby of the hotel, did not see Al Fleming, and tapped the bell. No one was in the bar, which was unusual for this time of evening, and the dining room was empty, but that was not unusual, because most people who took their meals in the hotel had supper close to six o'clock.

Fleming stepped into the lobby, saw who had rung the bell, and sighed in relief. He said: "Glad to see you, Sheriff. I was afraid it was somebody else."

"Who'd you expect?"

"Nobody in particular," Fleming answered, "but somebody who wanted John Brown sent on his way and would cuss me for giving him a room."

"Business seems a mite slim," Ed said.

"Slim?" Fleming snorted. "Hell, you'd think we had the plague, and you know why?"

"I can guess," Ed answered. "John Brown is a man to avoid, and folks are thinking he'd be around the hotel somewhere."

Fleming nodded. He did not seem as frightened as he had been in the afternoon, but he was still very nervous.

Ed studied him a moment, then asked: "You still jumpy about Brown being here?"

"I sure am," Fleming said. "I don't know why he's here, and I guess that's the reason me and a lot of other people are scared. If we just knew . . ."

His voice trailed off, as if he realized there was no way anyone could find out why John Brown was in Nugget City until he wanted them to know.

"Has he been around all evening?" Ed asked.

"He sat outside until it was dark," Fleming answered, "but I ain't seen him since he went up to his room. Didn't even go into the dining room for his supper. He ought to be plenty hungry by now."

Probably having supper with Cathy Allen, Ed thought, but he didn't mention it to Fleming. Instead he said: "Sam Thorn showed up a while ago and got after me to run Brown out of town. You saw how the women were. Just what is there about this gent that makes so many people worried about his being here?"

"I dunno about the others," Fleming said, "but I'll give you an honest answer as far as I'm concerned. It may be the same with Thorn, but I'm guessing the women are like a flock of hens when a hawk shows up. They get excited, whether the hawk is hungry or not. Women are like that, you know."

Ed didn't know, his knowledge of women being meager. Fleming was a bachelor, so Ed wondered how he knew so much about women. Maybe he could tell Ed why Cathy Allen was involved with a gunman, but he didn't pursue the subject.

46

"I could stand an honest answer on several questions," Ed said.

"I'll just answer one." Fleming glanced up the stairway, as if thinking Brown might be standing there listening, then he leaned toward Ed and lowered his voice as he said: "Suppose I had done something wrong years ago? Not here, but a long ways from here, and I came to Nugget to settle down and be safe. Sort of hide out, you know, with another name and a business. Then suppose this something I had done was to someone else, and this someone found out where I was living, so he sent a man here to kill me." He paused, glancing up the stairway again, and went on: "Now, I ain't saying I committed a crime, mind you, or that I am wanted by the law. I'm just saying that maybe I've been dogged by the fear that some day a killer would show up to pay me back for what I done."

Ed was surprised. Al Fleming was a meek man who wasn't the kind ever to harm anyone, but that didn't prove anything.

"You're saying that other people in town, like Sam Thorn, might think a killer was after him?" Ed asked. "And Thorn has settled down here, thinking he's in the clear, but then Brown shows up, and Sam gets very jumpy?"

"That's it," Fleming said. "Like I just said, I don't figure that's the case with the women, though some of them, like Missus Thorn, might know their husbands did something that could bring a killer after them. Now me?" He took a long breath. "I'll tell you the truth, Sheriff. I'm not wanted by the law, but I did do

47

something to a woman a long time ago . . . well, I didn't hurt her, but she had a passel of brothers who think I did, and they swore they'd kill me.

"I loved her, and I'm sure she loved me, but I was married to a woman I didn't love, so I was tied up and couldn't do anything about it. Well, this woman helped me get out of town, or I'd have cashed in my chips right then. I've never heard from her since, or heard anything about her."

He paused, looking across the street as if vividly recalling the scene from the past, and now was not seeing the street at all. He went on slowly. "I've traveled since then, made a little money, and kept on the move, so they'd never run me down, but, when I came here, I bought the hotel and settled down because not many strangers come to an old, worn-out mining town. But these brothers I mentioned are a tough bunch. They'll hate me as long as they live, so, if they ever find out where I am, they'll see I'm killed."

Fleming stopped talking and took a long breath. He was sweating, fetched a handkerchief from his pocket, and wiped his face. He felt better just because of the telling, Ed thought. Probably he had never told anyone else in all the years he'd been on the run.

Suddenly Fleming came out of the past and brought his gaze to Ed's face. "I'd appreciate it, Sheriff, if you didn't tell anyone what I just told you. I've tried to be a good citizen since I came here. I want people to trust and respect me. I think I have their trust and respect now, and I don't want them to think otherwise of me."

"Hell, I won't tell anybody," Ed said, "but I don't think you've got anything to worry about. If those brothers you mentioned were after you, they wouldn't send a man like Brown who advertises what he is by carrying two guns. It would be someone who didn't look or act like a killer, someone you would not suspect." He shook his head. "No, Brown's here for something else."

Fleming thought about it a moment, then nodded. "Sure, that makes sense. I guess I've been expecting somebody to show up for the last twenty years, and, when Brown got off the stage, I panicked, figuring this was the gent I'd been expecting."

"Thorn's a different case," Ed said thoughtfully. "If I'm any judge of a man, I'd say he was the kind who is wanted by the law somewhere, and he's been hiding out in Nugget City."

"And getting rich while he was doing it," Fleming said bitterly. "I never liked the bastard, but I owe him money, so I kowtow to him and hate myself for doing it."

Ed nodded, as if he understood, and turned to the door, saying over his shoulder: "I'll see you in the morning, Al," and left the hotel.

Ed's mother was asleep when he got home. At least she was in bed. She always called to him if she was awake when he came in, asking if everything was all right, but tonight her bedroom door was closed, and she didn't say anything. She had felt the tension of the day, he thought, and was exhausted.

He remembered how it had been when his father had been alive. She always worried about him when trouble was brewing, but oddly enough the more worried she was, the sooner she went to bed. Maybe she sought peace in sleep, he thought, or maybe she simply lay there, listening and worrying, and keeping it all to herself.

Ed went to bed, but he didn't sleep for hours. He might know tomorrow if Sam Thorn was involved, but Cathy Allen was different. Thorn would press him to run Brown out of town, but Cathy wouldn't say anything. He didn't want to ask her what she had to do with Brown's appearance in Nugget City, or ask Brown why he had waited until dark to slip into Cathy's house. They weren't likely to tell him the truth.

If they were up to some trickery, Ed knew he'd hear about it sooner or later, but that might be too late to stop them. That thought kept him awake for a long time, and it was close to midnight when he finally dropped into a troubled sleep.

CHAPTER
SEVEN

John Brown left Cathy Allen's house in the pre-dawn, slipping out through the back door. Before he left, he said: "I'll be back tonight as soon as it's dark."

"I'll have supper ready for you," she promised. "You stay out of trouble between now and then. And you sit in front of the hotel. I want Thorn to have lots of opportunity to see you."

"If you need me . . ."

"I'll yell," she said. "You watch for me to go into the bank. If I'm not out in fifteen or twenty minutes, you'd better come and see if I'm in trouble. I don't trust Thorn worth a damn."

"I'll watch," he said, and walked from the bedroom.

Cathy lay there a long time, thinking back over the night and enjoying in her memory every minute of it. Then her thoughts turned to Thorn, and she mentally pictured the expression that would be on his face when she told him she was blackmailing him, tried to imagine what he would say, and began to giggle. She wished that Mrs Thorn could be there to see and hear what went on.

Hunger finally drove her out of her bed long after the sun was up. She built a fire, made coffee, and returned to her bedroom to dress. She went to the kitchen, fried an egg, warmed up some biscuits, and sat at the table for a long time, drinking one cup of coffee after another as she rehearsed what she would say to Thorn.

She glanced at the clock on a shelf above the table and saw that it was half past eight. She took a long breath, knowing that Thorn was in the bank and that she was putting off what she had to do. She'd looked forward to it for a long time, always enjoying the scene as she pictured it, but, now that the time was here, she realized she might not enjoy it at all, that it might turn out to be a very dangerous situation.

She rose, leaving her dishes on the table, and, going into her bedroom, fussed with her hair until she had it exactly right, applied a little rouge to her cheeks, and headed for the front door. As she walked through the house, she saw Mrs Thorn's half-finished dress on the table and thumbed her nose at it.

"To hell with you," she said. "It won't be long until you'll wish I was back here, making your dresses."

She stepped out into the bright sunshine, moved briefly along the board walk to the business block, then crossed to the bank. The place was empty except for the cashier who looked up as she approached the gate at the end of the counter.

"Is Sam Thorn in?" she asked.

He nodded and rose. "I'll see if he can . . ."

"He can," she said. "I'll just go on in."

"You can't do that," he cried as he hurried toward her. "Mister Thorn always insists that his visitors be announced. Miss Allen, you can't go in . . ."

She had already pushed the gate back and reached the door to Thorn's private office a good three steps ahead of him. She opened the door and stepped into the room, slamming the door behind her and hoping that it plastered the cashier's nose against his face.

Thorn was working at his desk. When he heard the door open, he looked up, scowled, and called irritably: "Morgan, get this woman out of here."

"You'd better see me, Thorn," Cathy said, leaning against the door, "unless you want to die today."

The cashier was trying to shove the door open, and Cathy was trying to keep it closed. Thorn blinked a moment until her words registered in his mind, then he shouted: "Never mind, Morgan. I'll see her."

"That's better," Cathy said.

"Why didn't you let Morgan ask me if I would see you?" Thorn demanded. "That's the way we do things here. I don't like for you or anybody else to come . . ."

"I know how you do things," Cathy said, "and it was my guess that, if I'd let you do it your way, you wouldn't have had the time for me. Isn't that right?"

He picked a cigar out of the box on the desk in front of him and rolled it between his fingers as he stared at her. "Yes, that's right. Now, what's this business about dying today?"

She sat down in the chair across the desk from him, her eyes on his face. She decided it would be better strategy to lay her cards on the table now instead of holding back the threat of Brown's assistance. She had planned to use it only when it became necessary, but now, seeing the red color of his face that anger had given it, she realized she couldn't follow her plan.

"You've seen the gunman who came in on the stage yesterday?" she asked.

The red fled from his face. She sensed the feeling of anxiety that replaced the anger that had been in him. In the past he had simply rolled over anyone who opposed him, giving no apologies or excuses. Now, suddenly, he was not giving that impression at all. He was gripped by fear, a mortal man like everyone else.

"Yes," he said.

One word! No more. In that instant she knew she had the upper hand. She said: "That man is my future husband. He has a vicious temper, and he gets very angry when people hurt me in any way. He goes a little crazy. I advise you not to do anything that will arouse his anger."

"I see." He sat back in his chair, hands palm down on the top of his desk. "What do you mean?"

"I'm blackmailing you for ten thousand dollars," she said. "In cash. I will leave Nugget City as soon as the money is in my hands, and I will not tell anyone else what I know, not your wife or anyone. I'm sure that's the way you want it, and that you'll pay to keep it that way."

He began to tremble, his face turned white, and a muscle in his right cheek began pulsating with the regular rhythm of a heartbeat. He opened his mouth to say something, closed it, and seemed to choke. He swallowed with an effort, then asked in a low voice: "What do you know?"

"I know that for several months you have been sleeping with Sally York," Cathy said. "We both know she is not a good teacher and several parents have wanted to fire her, but you wouldn't stand for it. If they knew about you two, they'd understand why you've insisted on her staying."

He leaned back in his chair and blew out a long breath, almost smiling as he picked up the cigar and began rolling it between his fingers again. Suddenly panic swept through Cathy. He was actually relieved. He had expected something else, something far worse than sleeping with the school teacher. She wished she knew what it was, but she didn't, so she'd have to use the only weapon she had.

"I know you, Thorn," she said. "I know you are a proud man, proud of the respect the people of Nugget City have for you, but you and I know you are a damned hypocrite, and you'd better stop and figure on what folks will think of you once they know." She paused, her confidence returning as she pointed a forefinger at him. "If you don't pay what I'm asking, I promise you I'll march down Main Street and yell at the top of my voice that you've been sleeping with Sally York."

The smile that had threatened to break across his face a moment before did not materialize. He scowled, picked up the cigar, bit off the end, and put it into his mouth, then struck a match and held the flame to the end of the cigar.

"I wouldn't like that," he said as he puffed a great cloud of smoke into the room. "In fact, I can't let you do that. However, you are going to have to cut your demands. Five thousand is as high as I can go."

Cathy hesitated, remembering that $5,000 was all that she had expected to get out of him, but she knew she couldn't afford to give in too easily.

"I don't know," she said tentatively. "John and I talked it over, and he said we had to have ten thousand."

Thorn spread his hands, as if asking her to be reasonable. He said: "Miss Allen, I can't afford for the scandal you are threatening me with to come down on my head, but on the other hand I have to keep my bank accounts solvent. To do that, I must have a certain amount of money on hand to meet emergencies. I can let you have five thousand and keep my nose above water. Ten thousand would in all probability put me out of business. I will not let that happen. As painful as the scandal would be, I'd suffer through it rather than lose my bank."

What he was saying seemed reasonable to Cathy. She said: "We have a deal. I'll take the money, and we'll be out of town before noon."

"It's not that easy," he said. "I can't complete the transaction today. I simply don't have that kind of cash on hand, but I'll wire a bank in Gunnison and borrow it. The money will be on tomorrow's stage."

For a full minute she sat back in her chair, staring at Thorn. His face seemed expressionless now, and this surprised her after the fear and anxiety she had sensed a few minutes ago. She didn't like the feeling that swept through her. This wasn't quite right, and yet it still all sounded reasonable.

He said impatiently: "Well?"

It seemed to her that Thorn again was filled with the sense of power and self-assurance he usually was. She had a feeling he was lying, stalling for some reason that she couldn't put her finger on. He probably had plenty of money right here in his safe, but she had no way of proving that, so it seemed to her that she had no alternative but to play it his way. It was either that, or she'd have to make good on her threat and start yelling, and that meant no money at all.

She rose. "All right, Thorn, but I warn you. If you have an idea that you can weasel out of our agreement, you'd better forget it. John Brown has killed men before, and he would not hesitate for a minute to kill you if you forced the choice on him." She turned to the door, put a hand on the knob, then turned. "There is one more thing I'd better tell you. Besides having someone mistreat me, the one thing that John can't stand is a liar, a man who doesn't keep a promise."

She opened the door, stepped into the bank lobby, and crossed to the street door. She left the bank, feeling frustrated and uneasy. She had miscalculated somewhere. For a short time she'd had Thorn frightened to the point of panic and then, when she threatened him with exposure, he was no longer frightened. In fact, he actually seemed relieved.

She walked along the street at her usual brisk pace to the store where she bought meat for supper. Buck Moore was alone and, as he wrapped the meat, she said: "You had a crowd in here yesterday. Where'd they go?"

"Stayed home, I guess," he said sourly. "Damned women are like sheep. Missus Thorn panics and then the whole bunch take off in the same direction. Missus McCoy was the only one who showed a lick of sense."

She paid for the meat and picked it up. "Did she think Ed could handle the gunman if he had to?"

"I dunno about that," he said. "She kept telling 'em that the hardcase yonder hadn't done anything yet to scare folks." He shrugged. "Hell, Cathy, he ain't here to kill women, but you can bet on it he's here to kill somebody."

She smiled as she turned to the door, then paused to ask: "It wouldn't be you, would it, Buck?"

"I've made some enemies along the way," he said glumly, "and I've got skeletons in my closet like everybody else. I don't know why he's here, or who he's after, but I don't mind telling you I don't like him being in town."

She hesitated, wanting to tell him he had nothing to worry about. He was a kindly man who had given her credit when she first came to Nugget City, and she would have liked to spare him the worry that he plainly felt, but there was no way she could do that.

"I doubt that he's after you," she said and left the store, worried that, if she kept talking, she would say too much.

She returned home, noting that Brown was in front of the hotel as she had told him to be. She felt his questioning eyes on her, but she hurried on, giving no sign of recognition. There was nothing she could tell him. He'd have to wait until evening. She hoped he'd accept the agreement she'd made with Thorn. Actually, there wasn't much else he could do, but, if that money didn't come in on the stage tomorrow, there'd be hell to pay.

She cleaned up her breakfast dishes, swept the floor, made her bed. and found herself with nothing to do. She went outside and worked in her garden, determined that no matter how bored she was, she would not do a stitch on Mrs Thorn's dress. Then she thought about John and started to worry. He did indeed have a temper, and, if Thorn failed to keep his word, she didn't know what would happen.

All she knew for sure was that her dreams would be nothing more than dreams if Thorn failed to keep his word. She couldn't bear that. She had planned this too long and believed in it too much to accept failure. She refused even to consider that possibility. Thorn would come through with the money and be glad to get her off his hands and out of town.

Still, the doubts lingered. Finally she threw down her hoe and went into the house. She lay down on her bed and began to cry. She still felt that her estimate of Sam Thorn was right. He would do almost anything to keep the townspeople from knowing about him and Sally York. Yet the change in him had been too much to ignore. He must have thought of a way out of his dilemma, and she didn't have a guess what it was.

CHAPTER
EIGHT

Ed McCoy woke long after sunup. He lay in bed a few minutes, thinking about John Brown and Cathy Allen, finding the situation as puzzling as it had been the previous night. He heard his mother's Plymouth Rock rooster give out with a lusty crow, and then he was aware of the murmur of voices from the kitchen.

He rose and dressed, wondering who was calling. He left his bedroom and, crossing through to the front room to the kitchen door, stopped, shocked into immobility. Judy Maulden stood beside his mother at the kitchen range, their backs to him.

Instinctively he called: "Judy, when did you get here?"

She whirled, cried: "Ed," and ran into his arms.

For a long moment they stood holding each other, Ed shocked by her presence, Judy hungry for his love. Then Ed's mother said: "If you two can disentangle yourselves, we'll have breakfast. The eggs are about ready."

Judy stood motionless for a moment, her head tipped back, her eyes on Ed's face. "I've got a lot to tell you, but most of all I'm glad to be here."

"I'm glad you're here," he said. "Gladder than I can tell you."

He walked to the sink, filled a basin with water, washed, shaved, and combed his hair. When he turned toward the table. Judy was standing where he had left her, her eyes still glued to his face, as if she could not get enough of the sight of him. She was a medium-size girl with brown eyes and black hair, her face darkly tanned. She was at home on a horse as much as in the M Bar ranch-house kitchen, and could and had often worked as a cowhand when she was needed. Right now she was wearing Levi's and a man's shirt.

Under ordinary circumstances Judy bubbled over with good humor, but today her face was clouded with worry. Ed sensed that something had happened, and it certainly had not been good to bring her here so early in the morning.

"Sit down," Mrs McCoy said. "I hate cold eggs."

Judy flushed and moved to the table. She sat down. Ed took the chair across from her, and Mrs McCoy sat at the head of the table. She said to Ed: "I found her asleep on the back porch, curled up like a kitten."

"Why didn't you come in?" Ed demanded. "You know your way in this house."

Judy had lived with the McCoys while she was going to high school. Ed was older and at first resented her being here, calling her a tomboy, a pest, or a tagalong, but, before she finished school, he had fallen in love with her. As far as Judy was concerned, she contended she had loved him from the first day she had moved in. After she was graduated, she went back to the M Bar.

and he had not seen her as much as he wanted to because Curt Maulden demanded so much from her.

"I got here just a little before daylight," Judy said. "I thought it was better if I stayed outside. I knew I'd wake you up, if I went in, and maybe scare you, not knowing who it was."

Mrs McCoy passed the platter of fried eggs and bacon. She said: "You'd better tell him, Judy."

For a moment she busied herself, buttering a biscuit, then she said: "I guess you knew something like this would happen, Ed. That's why you wanted me to leave home and marry you. Well, I've left home, and I will marry you today or tomorrow or any day you say."

"That's the best news I ever heard," Ed said, "but what happened?"

"Curly Wilson was in town yesterday afternoon and saw the gunman who was sitting in front of the hotel," Judy answered. "He heard the gossip in the store, with nobody knowing why the man was here. He rode back home and told Pa. I wish he hadn't, but I guess any foreman would have told his boss what he'd heard. Probably Curly thought Pete Egan had sent for the man. Of course, Pa jumped to that conclusion as soon as Curly told him about the gunman." She paused, sipping her coffee, then went on: "Pa has been acting crazier'n ever. He'd been drinking a lot, too, which makes it worse. He's been threatening to cut off the water for years, but I never thought he'd really do it. After he heard about the gunman, he ranted and raved a while, then told Curly to finish the dam, starting work on it in the morning. You know most of it's been built for quite a while, so it's just a matter of filling in the middle."

"It won't hold water, will it?" Ed asked.

"It will for a while," Judy answered. "It will take several days for it to fill up. Pa wants it to get high enough to run out through the ditch he dug across the low part of the ridge that separates our valley from Judson's Cañon. What I think will happen is that, when the water gets high enough, it will take the dam out, and there'll be a wall of water going down the valley that will flood Nugget City."

Ed nodded somberly. "That's what I thought when I looked at the dam a year or so ago. I told Curt that, and he just laughed and said he hoped there was enough water to drown Pete Egan's cows."

"I've heard him say that," Judy agreed. "It's probably what he hopes will happen. He doesn't care how many people are drowned. That's how mean he's got." She shook her head. "He didn't used to be that way."

Ed went on eating, impatient to know what had happened to make Judy leave home but knowing she would tell it in her own time. Presently she said: "I heard him give Curly the order to finish the dam. I couldn't keep my mouth shut. I told him he couldn't do it, that people might be killed and their property destroyed, that it would bring the law down on him, and Pete Egan would be there with enough dynamite to blow the dam up." She stopped and sat, staring at the food on her plate, which she had hardly touched, then she went on: "He had a tantrum. He yelled that he'd never taken orders from a woman, and he wasn't going to start now, especially a girl who was too smart for her pants. I guess I yelled back at him and told him he was crazy if he did a thing like that." She took a long breath and glanced seriously at Ed. "I just plain lost my temper. It was the word crazy that set him off. I don't know if this is possible, but I think he's sane enough to be afraid that he is crazy. I know I shouldn't have said it, but I just couldn't hold my tongue. He hit me. It was a slap, but it was hard enough to knock me down. I wasn't hurt because I fell back on the couch."

Ed saw that she was close to crying and started to say she didn't have to tell the rest now, but she said quickly: "I've got to tell you, although there's not much left to tell. I'm not sure he'll go through with it, or if the crew will follow his orders. Lately Curly's been inclined to go ahead and do what has to be done and never tell Pa." She lifted the coffee cup to her mouth, set it back down, and shook her head. "That's about all there is to tell. I got off the couch and went into my room, and I knew I couldn't stay there any longer. I waited till he was asleep, then I got the key that opens the padlock on the gate. It was in his pants, but he was sleeping so soundly he didn't catch me. I left the house, saddled my horse, and left without waking anybody. I put my horse in your barn and, well, here I am."

"I wish I could see Curly," Ed said thoughtfully. "I might be able to talk some sense into him."

"I don't think you can say a word that would change Curly," Judy said. "If he does anything that isn't what Pa's ordered, it will be because he feels his way is better than what Pa wants done."

"We'll have to wait and see what Curly really does," Ed said. "When your pa's sober, maybe he'll be a little saner." He shoved his empty plate back, then he added: "I never did know exactly what the row with him and Pete Egan was all about. It's been going on as long as I can remember."

"It goes back to when you were little and before Judy was born," Mrs McCoy said. "I think you've heard it, but you've forgotten, and I doubt that Judy ever did hear the whole story. You see, both of 'em were in love with Judy's mother. Curt finally won her. He was a handsome man when he was young with a tongue dipped in honey, and he just plain fooled your mother, Judy. Fist and me didn't like Curt, but we couldn't tell your mother what we thought of the man she was in love with, or thought she was. I don't think she was ever happy after she married Curt. She died when you were so young, Judy, I don't suppose you remember her very well."

Judy nodded. "Vaguely. I remember most of the housekeepers a lot better than my mother."

"The point is that, when she died," Mrs McCoy went on, "Pete put out some ugly talk about how Curt had abused her and made her die young. Your mother used to come here and visit with me when she was in town, and I know some of the things that Pete said were true. Of course, Pete's talking made Curt wild, and he jumped Pete about it one day in a saloon, and they had a fist fight that folks talked about for months. Neither one licked the other. They just quit when they were so

65

exhausted that they couldn't fight any more. After that they more or less avoided each other.

"A year or so after that Pete made an agreement with all the butchers in Nugget City. I don't know how he wangled it, but he made them a special price that was a big saving to them and, of course, undercut what Curt would have charged. This added to Curt's bitterness because he had always sold beef to the local butchers."

"And now Pa blames Egan for losing his leg," Judy said.

Ed nodded, remembering how that had been. Maulden had been mounting his horse in front of the Silver Star Saloon when a bunch of the Rafter E boys rode in, yelling and shooting the way cowboys do sometimes when they ride into town. Maulden's horse started to buck. He was thrown across the hitch rail and splintered his leg so badly it had to be amputated. He claimed that Pete Egan started the shooting, hoping he'd make Maulden's horse do exactly what he did. As a matter of fact, Egan was not with his crew, but Maulden never believed it and swore that he'd square accounts with Egan some day.

Ed rose and went around the table to kiss Judy. He said: "I'm riding out to the Rafter E and have a talk with Pete. Maybe I'll go up the creek this afternoon and see your pa."

"No," she cried. "Don't do it. He'd shoot you before you got anywhere near the house. He keeps a Winchester right beside his chair."

Ed shrugged. "I'll see you as soon as I get back from talking to Pete. I want you to stay inside the house.

Don't let anyone know you're here. It's my guess your pa will send someone to town to bring you back."

She nodded. "I'm sure he will, and whoever he sends will come here before he looks anywhere else."

"Lock the door," Ed said. "I don't think anyone will smash the door down."

"I'll blow his head off if he tries it," Mrs McCoy said.

Ed left the house, knowing his mother would do exactly what she'd said she'd do.

CHAPTER
NINE

For several minutes after Cathy Allen left Thorn's office, the banker sat motionless as he pulled on his cigar. He had no intention of paying the Allen woman the money she had demanded. He'd had all he could do to keep from getting up and throttling her, and he would have, if it hadn't been for that gunslinger sitting in front of the hotel.

Cathy Allen had known she couldn't succeed in this blackmailing scheme without help, so she had sent for the gunman. It was no coincidence that he had showed up in Nugget City just before Cathy made her blackmail threat. Thorn had no idea what their relationship had been, but that wasn't important.

Cathy Allen must have been prowling the streets ever since she had come to town and had spied on him enough to know about him and Sally York. Well, he wasn't going to let her spoil what he had worked so hard to develop, and he wasn't going to give Sally up, either.

For a moment he thought of what his wife would say, if Cathy carried out her threat. He shuddered. Then he considered what the townspeople would say and that was worse. No, he couldn't let it happen, but on the other hand he didn't doubt what she'd said about him hearing from the gunman if he backed out of the deal he had made. Sam Thorn was a physical coward, and he knew it. He was strong when he dealt from strength, but on something like this he wouldn't have a chance against Brown, and he wouldn't even try.

For just a moment he remembered the fear that had paralyzed him when Cathy had started to talk, fear that some way or somehow she had learned of his past, a fear that had plagued him ever since he had come to Nugget City. A groundless fear, sure, but a fear that had been in him nevertheless. Then he thought of the relief that had poured through him when he'd heard what she did know. That was something he could handle. But how? If the gunman was removed, he could take care of the Allen woman. Then, suddenly, a decision came to him.

He opened a drawer, lifted a small metal box from it, and set it on top of his desk. He unlocked it, opened it, and counted out ten twenty-dollar gold pieces and five ten-dollar coins from the box, then closed and locked it. The box contained a special fund that he had saved so it would not have to be accounted for and could be used for just such emergencies as this.

Replacing the box in the drawer, he rummaged around until he found a small leather pouch, dropped the coins into it, then rose, slipped the pouch into his pocket, and left the office. As he crossed the bank to the front door, he said: "Morgan, I'm going to be gone most of the morning. If anything turns up that you

69

can't handle, say that I'll be in my office this afternoon."

"Yes, Mister Thorn," Morgan said in the subservient voice that he had learned pleased his boss.

Thorn left the bank, cigar still clutched between his teeth. He crossed the street to the hotel side and forced himself to walk in front of the gunman. He was no more than three feet from the man as he passed him, and for just an instant their eyes met, then Thorn hurried on. He did not look back until he reached the livery stable, and, when he did glance over his shoulder, he saw that the gunman had not moved.

The fellow was a tough. Thorn would picture that long-jawed, hard-eyed face in his dreams tonight. He wondered how Cathy Allen had met him. He had seen plenty of men like this one in Dodge City. They were a breed apart, men who could take a human life for no good reason except pay and do it without a trace of remorse.

Thorn stepped into the livery stable, and for the first time fear of the gunman began working its icy way up and down his spine. Now that he had seen the man's face close up, he realized more than ever how carefully the Allen woman had planned this. He had not really believed her as he had sat, listening to her threats. Well, the plan he had in mind had to work. It would cost him a few hundred dollars, but that was nothing like the amount the Allen woman was demanding.

The liveryman looked up from the stall he was cleaning when Thorn said: "Pat, harness Nellie and hook her up to my buggy."

70

The liveryman shrugged, leaned his pitchfork handle against the wall of the stall, and walked slowly along the runway to the stall that held the banker's mare. He worked deliberately, as if he had all day, and Thorn had to struggle to keep from yelling at him to get a move on.

Thorn realized he was sweating, that he was impatient, and he had to cool down. There wasn't a problem in the world he couldn't solve, he told himself, if he took his time and didn't panic. He had always gone on that premise, and it had worked. It just took time and a clear head.

The liveryman called: "All set, Mister Thorn."

He almost ran down the runway to where the mare and buggy waited, pulled himself into the seat, and, picking up the lines, drove out of the stable and into the street. He flicked his mare with the whip and left town at a trot, this time not even glancing at the motionless gunman.

He couldn't understand why Ed McCoy was reluctant to run the fellow out of town unless he was afraid he couldn't make it stick. That was probably the answer, although he had always respected Fist McCoy and had thought, or at least hoped, that young McCoy had inherited his father's guts. Well, there was always more than one way to skin a cat. Since he had not been able to get the law to do what he wanted, he'd have to fall back on money. More than once that had been his way of accomplishing something he wanted.

The last house fell behind, and he drove along the creek, the tall cottonwoods shading the road. Both sides of the valley sloped back gently, furnishing excellent winter pasture for Pete Egan's cattle. This was Rafter E range, all that Egan needed, but Thorn realized that the cattleman's greed was at least partly responsible for his feud with Curt Maulden. Thorn told himself that, if Egan had a brain in his head, he'd be satisfied with what he had, instead of reaching for the entire valley.

The road followed the creek until it came to the turnout to the Rafter E. A mile or so downstream the road to Gunnison angled upward over the steep ridge that formed the north wall of the valley. The creek roared through a gorge at this point, so narrow that there had been no room to build a road.

The turnoff to Egan's place split off to take a direct course up the side of the bench. Thorn's mare snorted and strained until she reached the top, and Thorn wondered, as he did every time he drove to the Rafter E, why Egan had not cut a road of switchbacks that would have made the climb much easier.

Another thing about Egan that bothered Thorn was the fact that he was not a man to save his money. He and his wife took extended vacations to California every winter. Mrs Egan spent far more for clothes than was necessary, and, when she had married Egan a few years before, she had demanded a grand house. He was often late with his interest, but Thorn never pushed him because he knew the rancher would pay sooner or later. The last thing he wanted to do was to irritate Egan.

The ranch buildings came into view as soon as Thorn reached the bench: the two-story frame house, the barn and outbuildings, and the picket fence, all painted white. It was a show place, but, before he was married, Egan always had money in the bank. He also had an unpretentious log house and a drab set of buildings and yard.

Ever since the man's marriage, Thorn had wondered how happy the cattleman was with a wife who never seemed satisfied with anything. She was, Thorn admitted to himself, a very pretty woman, but she had turned Egan's life around in a one-hundred-and-eighty degree revolution. She'd have to be a hell of a good bed-mate to compensate for what she had cost him.

Thorn thought about Egan's and Maulden's feud. It had gone back far beyond Egan's marriage, but Thorn was convinced that Mrs Egan had caused it to heat up. Certainly Egan had begun to covet Maulden's range in the south end of the valley only after his marriage. Maybe he always had wanted to expand, Thorn thought, but in recent years he had become more strident and had made more direct threats, claiming he lived in fear that Maulden would cut off his water. He had even attempted to buy Maulden's notes that the bank held.

Thorn had refused to sell the notes, mostly because he didn't want the feud to get any hotter than it was already. Besides, he had never had any trouble getting Maulden to pay his interest when it was due. He tried to get Egan to be less bellicose, but nothing he said changed Egan's attitude.

As he drove into the Rafter E yard, he glanced around. Egan was nowhere in sight, but Red Mike Kelso was hunkered down beside a corral gate, whittling. If Egan had seen him drive in, he probably thought the banker was here to press him about his interest which was overdue, so he was staying out of sight. Well, let him think what he wanted to. He was here to see Kelso, not Egan.

It had been typical of Egan to hire a gunfighter. He needed one about as much as he needed a case of typhoid fever. Hiring a man like Kelso was designed to frighten and worry Curt Maulden. Apparently it had worked. Certainly Maulden had become impossible to talk to once Kelso arrived in the valley.

Thorn drove up to within ten feet of Kelso and pulled his mare to a stop. He said: "Good morning, Red."

Kelso grunted and kept on whittling. His attitude infuriated Thorn who was used to getting respect from everyone in the county including Egan, but he was here to ask Kelso for a favor, so he held his temper. He stepped down from his buggy, the rig creaking as he transferred his weight to the ground.

"I understand you've hired your gun to Pete," Thorn said as he squatted beside Kelso. "I've never seen you draw a gun. Just how good are you?"

For the first time Kelso turned his head to look at Thorn, then he said sharply: "Good enough, if it's any of your business."

He was a young man, not much more than a kid. Twenty or twenty-one, Thorn guessed. His pimple-scarred face seldom showed expression of any kind. His eyes were light blue, the iciest eyes Thorn had ever seen, and he wondered if the man had feelings about anything.

74

"It is some of my business," Thorn said, "because I have a job for you."

Kelso shook his head. "I'm working for Pete."

"I know that," Thorn said, feeling his temper begin to boil up in him. He paused, waiting until he was sure he wouldn't say the wrong thing, then added: "I'm not aiming to interfere with your loyalty and sense of obligation to Pete. You can do what I'm asking in about one second, and it won't bother Pete in any way. There's five hundred dollars in it for you, half now and the rest when you finish."

Kelso stared at Thorn in his cold, expressionless way, then he asked: "What's the job?"

"A gunslinger packing two Forty-Fives showed up in town yesterday," Thorn said. "I want him killed." He paused, then added: "If you think you're fast enough to do it."

"I'm fast enough to take anybody," Kelso said, still staring at Thorn. "Why do you want him killed?"

"My business."

Kelso shrugged. "How do I do it?"

"He sits in front of the hotel all day," Thorn said. "It's up to you to find a way to work him into a gun fight."

"Let's see the color of your *dinero*," Kelso said.

Thorn tossed the sack that held the gold coins to him and said: "I want it done today."

Kelso opened the sack, counted the money, and nodded. "I'll do it. Just stay out of the way. I'll stop at the bank as soon as I'm finished."

Without another word Thorn rose, stepped into his buggy, and drove away. He wasn't as happy with the deal as he'd thought he would be. He had a creepy feeling, as if he had been handling a snake, and he had always hated and feared snakes. All he could do now was to hope that Red Mike Kelso was faster than the man with the two guns.

CHAPTER
TEN

Ed rode out of Nugget City in mid-morning, not knowing what he'd learn from Pete Egan. Chances were the rancher wouldn't tell him the truth. He'd probably deny sending for John Brown, so maybe this trip out to the Rafter E was a waste of time, but he had to try.

Getting in touch with Curt Maulden would be the next move. That, as Judy had said, might be impossible, but again he had to try. Somewhere along the line he'd come up with a reason for Brown's being here.

He hadn't been on the trail ten minutes when he saw Sam Thorn coming toward town in his buggy, the mare traveling at a fast clip. Once they came abreast, he started to raise a hand in greeting, but Thorn did not even glance in his direction. Staring straight ahead, the banker acted as if he hadn't seen Ed.

Pulling his horse to a stop, Ed hipped around in the saddle to stare at Thorn's back. He didn't expect the man to be friendly after their set-to the night before, but he didn't expect Thorn to ignore him, either. He sensed something different about the banker, the hard expression on his face, the unblinking eyes, staring straight ahead.

The man was worried, Ed thought. Or afraid. But why had he gone out to Egan's place? That had to be where he had gone. There wasn't anyone else to see out here except a few prospectors or a handful of ten-cow ranchers on the slopes above the valley. It was unlikely that any of them had business with the bank.

Ed rode on, thinking that he might find out from Egan what Thorn had wanted, or at least whether his visit had anything to do with Brown's presence in town. Ed shook his head in disgust. It seemed that every thought he had eventually involved Brown — and damn it, Brown wasn't that important. Or was he? Ed had to admit that Brown's presence was like yeast working in a batch of dough.

When he reached the Rafter E ranch house, he saw that Red Mike Kelso was hunkered down in front of a corral gate. The gunman ignored him. After staring at him for a moment, Ed turned toward the front door. Before he reached the porch, Egan flung the door open and stepped onto the porch.

"Come in, you old horse thief," Egan bellowed. "Come in and we'll get the missus to pour you a cup of coffee."

"Howdy, Pete," Ed said, grinning. "I'll just do that."

Pete Egan was a squat man, his face a map of Ireland. He could explode into anger one moment and be affable the next. The one exception was anything that related to Curt Maulden about whom he was never affable. Ed was aware that Egan was often a seething volcano when he appeared very calm, but generally speaking Ed got along well with the rancher.

One thing was sure. Ed was not going to tell Egan what Judy had said about her father's ordering the completion of the dam. That would be all the spark it would take to set off the explosion that had been threatening for so long.

Egan stepped aside and motioned for Ed to go into the house. Egan followed, closing the front door behind him. Then he yelled: "Flower, fetch the sheriff a cup of coffee." He indicated a massive leather chair for Ed to occupy as he asked: "What fetches you out here today? I never knew you to ride this far just to pass the time of day."

"Oh, I've got some business, all right," Ed said, "but first I've got a question that you sure don't have to answer, because it ain't none of my business, but was Sam Thorn here a little while ago?"

Egan sat down in a rocker and, taking the makings from his vest pocket, rolled a smoke. He said: "It's funny you'd ask."

"I passed him on the road going back to town," Ed said. "He acted strange, like he didn't see me. I figured something was wrong."

"He was here, all right," Egan said after he'd lit his cigarette, "but the funny part is I can't tell you why he was here. I saw him drive up in his buggy. I'm behind in my interest to the bank, so I figured he was here to raise hell about it. I was surprised because he's always been real good about that, letting me pay when I can.

"Well, I didn't want to see him, so I stayed yonder by the window, thinking that if he wanted to see me that bad, he'd have to come to the house and knock, but he didn't come to the house. He drove over to where Red Mike was and got out of his buggy. Mike was where he is right now by the corral gate. They talked, then Sam got back in his buggy and left." Egan paused, his eyes on Ed. "My God, Sheriff, I wish I knew why he came out and what he said to Mike."

"I didn't figure Mike ever had any business with the bank," Ed said.

"I didn't, either," Egan agreed, "but maybe it went the other way. Maybe Sam had business with Mike. Oh, there was another thing. Before he left, Sam gave Mike something. I couldn't see what it was. Might have been money."

Ed shook his head. "What would Sam hire Kelso for? He ain't good for anything except killing people, and I ain't sure how good he is at that."

"He ain't worth a damn when it comes to work," Egan admitted morosely. "He ain't turned a hand since he got here, but that ain't nothing for me to criticize him for. I didn't hire him to work."

Mrs Egan came in with a tray. She set it on a stand beside Ed and made a great ceremony out of pouring coffee into a small china cup. A sugar bowl and cream pitcher were on the tray. They were very thin and fragile with tiny blue flowers around the rim. She carefully picked up the cup, set it in a saucer, and offered them to Ed, asking: "Do you take cream and sugar?"

"No thanks," Ed said, accepting the cup and saucer and holding them gingerly.

"I'll leave the tray here, Sheriff," she said, "so you can pour more coffee for yourself, if you want it."

She was a small woman with delicate features and an air of what Ed thought royalty would have. She was close to her husband's age, but she contrived to look younger. Her long, blonde hair was braided and pinned to the back of her head, with a tiny pink ribbon somehow worked into the braid. She wore a pearl necklace and had two rings with large diamonds on her fingers. For a moment she stood smiling at him, wanting to be noticed, then turned, her light green silk dress rustling as she made her pivot toward the kitchen. She left the front room in short, mincing steps, confident, Ed thought, that he was watching her. She was wearing a fortune, Ed told himself, a fortune big enough to pay off her husband's debts.

Ed had trouble getting his big fingers around the handle of the cup, but, when he succeeded in getting a firm grip, he gulped the coffee, then set the cup back into the saucer, and placed both on the tray, relieved that he hadn't spilled the coffee on the oriental rug.

He glanced around the room, noting all the oil paintings on the wall, the rosewood piano set against the far wall, and the solid oak furniture, then looked at the rug, thinking that his mother was happy with the rag rugs that covered her floors. To Ed, the feeling in the room was one of absolute luxury and didn't seem to fit Pete Egan, the Pete Egan he had known as a boy. He had noticed that the man's eyes were on his wife all the time she was in the room, quietly worshipping her, so he probably had not regretted his bargain.

"Well?" Egan demanded. "What did you ride out here for? If you're trying to tell me that Curt Maulden has recovered his sanity . . ."

"I wish I could tell you that," Ed interrupted, "but I sure wouldn't try to tell you anything about Curt Maulden, so don't start harping on him. I'm out here because a gunfighter rode into town yesterday on the stage. I don't know a thing about him except that he calls himself John Brown. As far as I can tell, he's not a wanted man. At least I don't have a reward dodger on him. He sits in front of the hotel all the time except when he's asleep. Far as I know, he didn't even eat his supper in the hotel."

"What's that got to do with me?" Egan demanded.

"Maybe nothing," Ed said, "but it raises a question in my mind. Did you send for him?"

"Hell, no," Egan shouted angrily. "Why the hell should I? I hired Mike Kelso against the time I root that son of a bitch of a Maulden out of his hole and take the M Bar over. Why should I hire two gunfighters?"

"That's all I wanted to know," Ed said as he rose. "Thank your wife for me for the coffee."

"Maybe Maulden hired him," Egan said. "By God, if he has, I'll . . ."

"Let's find out if he has before you make a move," Ed said.

He walked to the door and paused there, as Egan said: "I thought a hell of a lot of your pa, and I've always liked you. I sure don't want no trouble with you, but everything I've got is wrapped up in this spread.

82

Without water, it ain't worth a damn. Sooner or later Maulden is gonna cut it off. He's threatened to often enough. When he does, I'm moving in with Mike Kelso and my whole outfit, and I'm gonna wipe the M Bar off the face of the earth, then I'll dicker with Judy and buy the outfit. I'm gonna have it, Ed, and don't try to stop me."

"I'll stop you, Pete," Ed said. "If Curt does cut off the water, and I know he's loco enough to do it some time, I'll go after him, but, if you don't stay inside the law, I'll come after you, too."

Egan grinned wryly. "You've got a lot of old Fist in you, boy, and that's all to the good. I tell you what. There'll be no trouble between you'n me if you use me and my boys as deputies."

Ed's first reaction was to say to hell with you, I don't need deputies, but he knew he would, and he didn't know where he'd find them in town, so he said: "We'll see," and left the house.

He crossed the yard to his horse, untied him, and stepped into the saddle. He sat there motionless for a moment, eyeing Kelso, then he rode toward him. Reining up, Ed continued to stare at the man who appeared to be completely unaware of his presence.

"I hear Thorn drove out to see you," Ed said.

Kelso looked up then, his eyes defiant. "Can't a man have a visitor without the law poking its long nose into his business?"

"It might be my business, too," Ed said, a growing conviction in his mind that he knew why Thorn had driven out here. "I know how men like you think.

You've got to be top dog, and now there's a new man in town who threatens you. You've got to find out if he's as fast as you are."

"So." Kelso got to his feet. "That's natural, ain't it?"

"Not to me, it ain't," Ed said, "and it sure as hell ain't worth a killing. I don't aim to have one in my bailiwick. Those things happened in my dad's time, but not in mine."

"You gonna stop it?" Kelso asked, his tone a challenge.

"I aim to, if that's what Thorn came out here for," Ed said sharply. "Was it? Did he promise to pay you if you try to kill Brown?"

"Try to?" Kelso sneered. "I'm going to. He's got no business here. As to what Thorn wanted, it ain't none of *your* business."

Kelso was young and brash and filled with contempt for any kind of authority. Ed had disliked him from the day he had come to the valley, and Kelso had done nothing to change that dislike. Now, his eyes locked with those of the young gunman, it was all Ed could do to keep from stepping down and giving him a lesson in courtesy, but he had learned one important thing when he'd pinned on the star: he did what he had to do but only at the right time.

Ed leaned forward in the saddle as he said slowly: "If you get out of line, Kelso, you'll find out how far my business goes."

He reined his horse around and left at a gallop, his temper at a boiling point. He had cooled down by the time he reached the creek and slowed his horse to a walk, wanting to think about what was happening and sort events out into some sort of pattern, but he could not. There were too many questions.

Ed did not doubt that Thorn had paid Kelso to kill Brown. But why? Thorn was never known to spend his money foolishly. Wanting Brown out of the valley was one thing, paying to have him killed was something else. There had to be several facts that Ed didn't know, missing pieces of the puzzle, but he had a feeling that he wouldn't find them in time to stop the trouble that certainly lay ahead.

He rode into town, thinking it was the same old story with a lawman. He was helpless until an overt act had been committed, and then it was too late. As he thought about it, he decided that he had at least learned one thing by riding out to the Rafter E. Pete Egan had not sent for John Brown. That brought up the next question. Was Curt Maulden responsible for Brown's presence in the valley?

CHAPTER
ELEVEN

Judy and Mrs McCoy sat at the table, drinking coffee until the pot was empty. Judy was hungry for woman talk, having lived with men so long that she had forgotten what it was like to just sit and visit with another woman, but this was more than that. She was a young woman who had almost no memory of her mother and now needed a surrogate mother to fill the void.

Finally Mrs McCoy sighed and rose. "I guess we'd better try to do the dishes, Judy. Everything's so dried on them by now, we may just have to throw them away."

"Oh, I guess I can get them cleaned up." Judy rose and, going around the table, hugged Mrs McCoy. "You don't know how good it feels just to be here again and be able to talk to you."

"You're so precious," Mrs McCoy said. "I always wanted a daughter, but, after Ed came, the doctor said that was it. No more children."

"I'm going to be your daughter as soon as Ed and I can marry," Judy said.

"Oh, I'll warrant that will be right soon," Mrs McCoy said, laughing. "You don't know how impatient he's been. I reckon he may want to put it off a bit because he's worried about what's going on around here. He wouldn't want you to be a young widow. But I don't think it'll be very long."

"Well," Judy said passionately, "if I could choose the day, I'd say this afternoon. I'd rather be a young widow than not to have had him at all."

Mrs McCoy didn't say anything for a time. She poured hot water from a tea kettle into a dishpan, then cooled it with cold water from the pump, and filled a second pan with rinse water. Judy stacked the dishes and brought them to the back of the stove. Mrs McCoy scrubbed them, muttering about nothing being worse than dried egg yolk, then slid each dish into the rinse pan.

"I know the way you feel, Judy," she said finally. "I felt the same way when I was a girl and in love with Fist, but he was stubborn, so I think you will have to wait a few days."

"But a sheriff never would get married if he waited for a time when he'd be safe so his wife wouldn't be a widow," Judy cried.

"I know that," Mrs McCoy agreed, "but right now things are different with that gunman in town. Nobody knows what he's up to, and it doesn't seem like it could be any good."

Judy sighed. "I'll need time to make a wedding dress, so maybe it would be better to wait a little while. I guess I'm afraid that Pa will find a way to make me come back. And, anyhow, we don't have a place to live."

"Like I told you," Mrs McCoy said, "you're welcome to stay here, but I know you'll want your own place. There's a lot of truth in the old saying that no kitchen is big enough for two women, even women who love each other. Of course, you'll want your own house. I'll be lonely, but I'll try to stay out of yours and Ed's business."

Judy laughed uncertainly. "Don't try too hard. I'm used to running a house for a bad-tempered father, but I might have trouble taking care of a house in town."

"There's one thing that will keep you and Ed busy for a while," Mrs McCoy said. "Any house you rent will have to be cleaned up before you can live in it. These vacant houses haven't been lived in for years, so any one of them you pick will need painting and papering and probably some shingles and windows."

"I can help Ed," Judy said. "It will be fun to be doing something together."

"And another thing," Mrs McCoy said, thinking she'd better tell Judy the facts of life as far as Ed was concerned, "he doesn't have much money. His salary is mighty piddling in a small county like this. It will be tough sledding for a married man."

"Maybe I can find something to do after we get settled," Judy said. "I'd like to teach, but I suppose they'll keep Sally York."

"I don't know about that," Mrs McCoy said angrily. "She's not a good teacher, and I don't know of any parent who likes her."

"You know Sam Thorn was the one who got our high school closed. Sure, it was small like he said, but it was our school, and kids could go there when they couldn't afford to pay room and board in Gunnison."

Mrs McCoy nodded. "And now all we have is a one-room school with too many kids for one teacher."

"Thorn claimed it would save the district a lot of money," Judy said. "Maybe it has, but saving money isn't the only thing to be considered. He came right out and said, if some people didn't have the money to send their children to Gunnison, their kids could go without an education."

"He's such a pious man," Mrs McCoy said sarcastically. "It's hard to understand how there can be so much difference between what he says and pretends to be, and what he actually is." She sighed, adding: "At least we've managed to stay out of debt to him."

"That's more than Pa's done," Judy said. "The M Bar has fallen behind for several years."

"Probably because your pa isn't able to get out and run things," Mrs McCoy said.

"I guess so," Judy agreed. "I think we would have been all right if Pa would have left everything to Curly, but he thinks he knows more than Curly does. The trouble is he can't ride out on the range and see for himself how the grass is, so he says that's the way it's always been and the way we'll keep doing things. Of course, each year is different, and what was right a year ago isn't always right this year."

Mrs McCoy threw the dish water out through the back door, then returned, wiping the pan with a dish cloth. "About our furniture, Judy. I have more in this big house than I'll need after Ed leaves. It's not new by a long shot, and I guess a bride always wants new things, but you're welcome to take what you need until you're able to buy what you want."

"I'm one bride who doesn't have to have new furniture," Judy said. "I'll be happy . . ."

A heavy pounding on the front door interrupted her. She looked at Mrs McCoy, a hand coming up to her throat as her heart began to pound. She whispered, "I'm guessing that's somebody from the M Bar wanting me come home. I won't do it. I'm never going back."

"You stay here," Mrs McCoy said. "I'll go look through a window and see who it is."

She left the kitchen and returned a moment later. "It's Curly Wilson. I'll tell him you're not here."

"No," Judy breathed. "Don't lie for me. Just tell him I'm not going back."

Mrs McCoy hesitated, then said reluctantly: "All right, I'll tell him, but it ain't going to satisfy him."

She crossed the front room to the door and opened it. Wilson stood there, a fist lifted to rap again. When he saw Mrs McCoy, he raised his hat from his head, saying: "Morning, Miz McCoy. I'm looking for Judy."

He was a tall, very thin man, about forty, bowlegged and deeply tanned from his years of forking a horse and being exposed to wind and sun. His head was totally bald, which often provoked jests such as having been scalped by the Utes the day he was born. He was, everyone agreed, a top hand, and the only question anyone ever raised about him was why he continued to work for a bastard like Curt Maulden, but he had ridden into the valley as a boy when Maulden brought his herd across the mountains and had worked for him ever since. Bonds of loyalty held him to the M Bar, though they had been severely tested many times.

"I'm sorry, Curly," Mrs McCoy said. "Judy told me she doesn't want to talk to you."

Mrs McCoy slammed the door shut, but Wilson pounded on it again, and, when she opened the door a second time, he said: "I'm sorry, Miz McCoy, but I can't go back without seeing her. The old man would kill me if I did."

Mrs McCoy started to shut the door again, but Wilson shoved a boot against the door and kept her from closing it, shouting: "I tell you, I've got to see her."

In exasperation Mrs McCoy grabbed a shotgun from the antler rack near the door, broke it to see that it was loaded, cocked it, then threw the door wide open and jammed the muzzle of the gun against Wilson's stomach.

"Let us alone, Curly," Mrs McCoy yelled, "or I'll blow your goddamned head off."

Wilson held his ground, grinning at her. "Ma'am," he said, "that ain't where my head is."

The anger went out of Mrs McCoy, and in spite of herself a smile touched the corners of her mouth. Behind her Judy called: "Let him in. I'll talk to him."

Mrs McCoy stepped back, the shotgun held on the ready. "All right. Talk. Then you vamoose, and, if you try anything funny, I will blow your head off, and I'll hold the gun in the right place next time."

Wilson stepped into the room. "Thank you, ma'am," he said, and turned to Judy who was standing in the kitchen doorway. "Your pappy wants you to come home, Judy. He says he don't know what to do with you gone."

"I'm never coming home," Judy said sharply. "I don't even think of the M Bar as my home any more."

He stood motionless in the center of the room, holding his hat by the brim and turning it slowly. He said: "Judy, I was in the house the night you were born. I've watched you grow up into a mighty purty girl. I know you've taken a hell of a lot from your pappy, and I don't blame you for running away. But if you'll come back, it'll be different. I promise you. If it ain't, I'll help you leave."

She shook her head. "I'm sorry, Curly. There's not going to be a next time. I wouldn't go back for anything or anybody. I'm going to marry Ed."

"Can't blame you for that, either," Wilson said. "Ed's a good man, but we need you on the M Bar. We all need you."

"You'd best go, Curly," Mrs McCoy said. "You've had your say, and you've heard what Judy has to say. She ain't gonna change her mind, so git."

Wilson shook his head stubbornly. "I can't do that, Miz McCoy. If you're bound to blow my head off, go ahead. You see, Curt ain't hisself." He paused, then asked: "Judy, why did you leave?"

"He hit me," Judy said. "If I went back, he might kill me."

"No, he wouldn't do that," Wilson said. "He was a fool, and he's sorry. He ate with the crew this morning. He was crying, Judy. He was just kinda out of his head. I figger he'll never be right again if you don't come back. He sets a store by you."

"I don't believe it," Judy snapped. "I don't think he ever loved me. He never acted like he did. I don't remember him hugging or kissing me, or even saying anything nice. When I finished high school and went back, I was useful because he could fire his housekeeper." She paused and drew a long breath. "Curly, I know I shouldn't say this, but I hate him."

The corners of Wilson's mouth started to twitch. He tried to say something, but his words seemed to choke him. Judy crossed the room to him and put an arm around him. She said: "Curly, you've always been special to me. After we're married, I want you to come and visit us, but I can't and won't go back to the M Bar."

He hugged her with one arm as he raised the other arm and swiped a hand across his face. "You're a good girl, Judy. You turned out better than we had any right to expect, being raised by housekeepers the way you was. And Curt, being kind of whacky all the time. He's getting worse. You've been about all that's kept him sane. If you don't come back, I don't think he'll ever be right again."

"He won't be right again whether I go back or not," Judy said, her voice showing the irritation that was beginning to rise in her. "I can't keep him sane. He's going to finish the dam and cut Pete Egan's water off. come hell or high water. That's crazy, Curly."

"I reckon it is," Wilson said, "but that ain't what I'm trying to tell you. We all love you, Judy. There ain't a cowhand on the spread who wouldn't do anything for you."

Judy whirled and walked back into the kitchen.

Mrs McCoy said: "We've been real patient with you, Curly. Now you git before I git more impatient than I am."

"All right," Wilson said, and reluctantly turned to the door.

CHAPTER
TWELVE

When Ed was still a block from the McCoy house, he recognized Curly Wilson's big sorrel, tied in front. He was surprised, then angered, for he remembered Judy's saying that her father would probably send someone to get her. He cracked steel to his horse, rode the last block in a hard run, and pulled up in a cloud of dust.

He swung down and started running toward the front door just as it opened and Wilson came out of the house. Mrs McCoy stood a few feet inside the door with a shotgun in her hands. Instinctively Ed drew his gun, shouting: "What are you doing here, Curly?"

"I came to see Judy," Wilson said. "Put your gun up. Nobody's hurt."

"It's all right, Ed," his mother said as she stepped onto the porch. "We've just been talking."

Ed looked from Wilson to his mother and back to Wilson, not satisfied with what he was hearing. He said: "I want to see Judy."

Mrs McCoy called over her shoulder: "Judy, Ed wants to see you."

They stood that way for a moment, a frozen tableau until Judy joined Mrs McCoy. She stopped, apparently realizing this was an explosive situation, then stepped off the porch, and walked quickly to where Ed stood just inside the picket fence that surrounded the McCoy front yard.

"Curly came to ask me to go back to the M Bar," Judy said, a hand on Ed's right arm. "Put your gun back into your holster. I told him I wasn't going back." Suddenly she threw her arms around Ed and hugged him. "I'm so glad you're back all in one piece. We've been worried." She turned to Wilson. "He's been out to the Rafter E, and with that crazy Red Mike Kelso there we were afraid something would happen."

Wilson showed his surprise. "Well?" he asked. "Did anything happen?"

"Nothing," Ed answered.

Wilson walked to his horse, untied him, then said: "I want to talk to you, Ed. I'll buy you a drink, if you've got time."

Looking at Judy, Ed hesitated, still not satisfied with the situation. "Yeah, I've got time, but I want to talk to Judy first. You go ahead."

"I'll meet you in the Bull's Head," Wilson said.

He mounted and rode away. Ed and Judy stood watching him, until he turned a corner and was out of sight, then Ed drew Judy to him and kissed her hard. From the porch Mrs McCoy said: "I seem to always be trying to separate you two lovebirds, but I want Ed to come in for a cup of coffee."

They walked into the house arm in arm, Ed saying: "Looks to me like I was the one who had better do some worrying. What were you doing with that shotgun, Ma?"

She replaced the gun on the antler rack, then said: "I didn't need it, but I thought I might. Curly got a little rambunctious, pounding on the door and yelling that he had to see Judy, so I opened the door and kept the shotgun on him. I didn't aim to let him in the house, but Judy said she'd talk to him." She jerked her head at Ed. "Come on into the kitchen. I've just put a pot of coffee on the stove."

"What did you talk about?" Ed asked. "Seems like all it would take was for you to tell him no."

"Oh, I told him, all right," Judy said. "He was hard to convince. He kept begging me to come back."

"I felt a little sorry for him," Mrs McCoy said as she poured the coffee. "He kept saying they all needed Judy, that it would never happen again with her pa, and that he'd never be right if she didn't come home."

"I never saw Curly like that before," Judy said. "He's not one to beg anybody for anything. He's always been kind to me." She hesitated, frowning thoughtfully. "Now that I think about it, I guess I would say he's been affectionate, certainly more than Pa ever was. He'd pat me on the back, or just touch me and tell me I was pretty." She hesitated again, staring at the wall as if she didn't see it. "You know, Ed, when you're growing up with a housekeeper who doesn't care anything about you and a father who takes you for granted and a crew of rough men who don't know how to act around a woman, it was kind of nice to have someone show a little affection."

Ed sat down at the table and sipped his coffee, more uneasy about Wilson's visit than he wanted Judy to know. He asked: "Curly threaten you?"

Judy shook her head. "Oh no. He said Pa was sorry he hit me, though I doubt that. I don't think he's sorry at all. I'm guessing Curly just said that to get me to come back."

"He said they all needed her," Mrs McCoy said. "You think they felt that, Judy? I mean, seems like they wouldn't have seen that much of you."

"Oh, I don't know," Judy said thoughtfully. "They saw me around the ranch a lot. I even helped out sometimes, like at roundup. Maybe they just like seeing a woman around."

"I can savvy that, all right," Ed said as he set his cup on the table. "I'd better go see what Curly has on his mind." He hesitated, then he added: "I don't want to scare you, Judy, but did Curly give you any hint that they would kidnap you or do something to make you go back?"

"Oh, no," Judy said quickly, shaking her head. "They wouldn't do that."

"I wouldn't bank on it," Ed said. "I don't like it worth a damn." He turned to his mother. "We'd better think of some place we can take her where she'd be safe, some place they wouldn't think of looking for her."

"They wouldn't think of looking on the Rafter E," Mrs McCoy said.

"Are you crazy?" Ed demanded. "Put her in Pete Egan's hands? She'd be a hostage. Pete . . ."

"Oh, I'm not that crazy," Mrs McCoy interrupted. "I was thinking of the Abbots. They live on Rafter E range. They'd be glad to take her."

Ed thought about that a moment. Monk Abbot had been a deputy and a close friend of Fist McCoy's for years. When he was no longer needed, he and his wife took a quarter section up Kaiser Cañon. He kept a milk cow and some chickens, and worked part time for Egan when he was needed, but mostly he lived off the country. Kaiser Cañon was part of Rafter E's range. Egan let him and his wife alone as long as he didn't try to run cattle.

"It might be a good idea," Ed said. "Missus Abbot would love to have her. You know them, don't you, Judy?"

"I know who they are," Judy said. "You're imagining things, Ed. I'm safe here."

"We'll see," Ed said. "You stay inside."

"Oh, I'll do that," Judy agreed, "although I don't think that's necessary, either."

Ed left the house, mounted, and rode the block and a half to the Bull's Head. He stepped down and tied beside Wilson's sorrel, noting that John Brown was seated in his usual place in front of the hotel. Ed told himself he couldn't sit there for hour after hour the way the gunman was doing. Brown was at least a very patient man. Then, too, maybe he was tired, tired of running from the law or from someone who was on his trail, and he wanted to be in position to see anybody who showed up in Nugget City. As he turned toward the batwings, Ed thought that he still had no real idea what the man was like, not even whether he was fast with his gun. Carrying two .45s didn't prove a thing.

When Ed entered the saloon, he saw Wilson sitting at a back table. He nodded at the bartender and strode on to where Wilson sat. A bottle and two glasses were on the table, one empty, one partly full.

"Sit down." Wilson nodded at the chair across from him and lifted the bottle to pour Ed's drink, but stopped at Ed's wave of the hand. "What's the matter? It's good whiskey."

"I ain't questioning that," Ed said, "but I don't drink when I've got problems, and right now I've got a dozen of 'em. I got 'em the minute that jasper up the street got down off the stage yesterday. I still haven't figured out how a man can kick up so much hell and not do a damn' thing."

"He's a tough-looking gent," Wilson said. "Been sitting there ever since he got to town?"

"Just about. I guess he didn't sleep in that chair, but he's sure been sitting in it most of the time."

"It ain't natural."

"It ain't for a fact," Ed agreed. "It drives me loco, trying to figure out what he's up to."

"He's got a reason for sitting there," Wilson said. "You can count on that. When I first seen him, I figgered Egan had sent for him, but, if that's the case, I can't see why he's sitting there like that. Looks like he'd have got hisself a horse and rode out to the Rafter E before this."

100

"Pete claimed he didn't send for him," Ed said. "I don't think he was lying. He believes Curt sent for him."

Wilson laughed softly. "Well, he didn't. I can tell you that. Before I leave town, I'm going to offer that gunslinger a job. I wouldn't be so sure Pete wasn't lying to you. Lying comes easy to him. If this gunslinger turns me down, you can make a good guess that he is working for Egan, and he's just watching what goes on around here."

Ed shook his head. "Pete ain't that anxious to know what goes on in this town. Now, if Brown was up the creek, watching you finish Curt's dam, I'd say you were guessing right."

Wilson shrugged and let it go at that. He picked up his glass and squinted at it, frowning. "Funny thing about a glass of whiskey. I just poured it before you came in. Now look at it. Half empty."

"No it ain't," Ed said, grinning. "It's half full."

Wilson chuckled. "I thought you'd say that. You see, it's all in a man's point of view. It's that way with Judy. You figure she belongs to you and that you're gonna marry her, but me'n Curt, along with everybody else on the M Bar, allow that she ought to be home. We miss her, Ed. We miss her like hell. It just wasn't right around there this morning. Curt came out and ate with us in the cook shack. That's how we knew she was gone."

"She's a grown woman, Curly," Ed said. "She's got a right to live her own life and make her own decisions. She sure ain't been treated right by Curt. I told her more'n a year ago she ought to leave home. Now, after hitting her the way he did, she's afraid of him."

"It'll be different when she comes back," Wilson said. "I'll guarantee it. I'll crack Curt's head wide open if he ever lays a hand on her again."

"Damn it, he ain't gonna get a chance to," Ed said hotly. "She ain't going back. It's her decision. She's not a child."

"I know that." Wilson finished his drink and set his glass on the table. "You see, folks think Curt's crazy. He ain't. He's just crazy as far as Pete Egan's concerned. Otherwise, he's as sane as you or me. That's where Judy comes in. I guess you'd call her a balance wheel. Curt sort of teeters back and forth on the edge of being clean crazy, and Judy's been the one who's kept him from tipping over. But there's more to it than that. You see, Curt ain't her father."

Ed's mouth fell open in astonishment. "Then who is?"

"Curt thinks he is," Wilson went on. "If you ever tell anyone what I'm going to tell you, I'll kill you. That's a promise."

"I won't agree to anything," Ed said, "and we'll see about you killing me, but I'm asking you again . . . who is her father?"

Wilson picked up his empty glass and began turning it slowly with the tips of his fingers, then he said in a low tone: "I am."

CHAPTER
THIRTEEN

Ed would not have been more amazed if Wilson had said the sun was sinking in the east. He stared at the man, too shocked to say anything for a moment, then he whispered, "I don't believe it."

Wilson shrugged. "Believe what you damn' please, but it doesn't change the truth. Curt never could have children. His wife didn't know that when they were married. When she did find out, she was pretty bitter because she wanted children, but that didn't have anything to do with what happened between us.

"It wasn't long after they were married. I don't reckon you were old enough to remember her, but she was a beautiful woman and a fine lady. They ain't always the same. She deserved better than Curt for a husband. I reckon even Pete Egan would have given her more happiness than Curt ever did. Well, I was purty young then, about her age, I guess, and was kind of a chore boy around the M Bar. Leastwise I got all the dirty jobs no one else wanted.

"It happened one fall when Curt was gone with the crew for several days. They were taking a herd to Gunnison to ship to Denver. Miz Maulden always did a lot of work around the yard, flowers and a garden and such, so that day I was working for her, and with Curt being gone and all ... well, it just happened. No scheming or anything. It never happened again. I was sure willing, but she was kind of ashamed, I guess."

Wilson had been staring at his empty whiskey glass as he talked. Now he filled it, downed his drink, and laid his gaze on Ed's face. "I don't want Judy to know. When you grow up thinking one man is your pa, and then find out somebody else is, it's gonna play hell with the way you feel, especially a girl like Judy. I'm telling you this because I want her back on the M Bar. I want her where I can see her and know how she's getting along. If she married you, hell, I'd never see her." He leaned forward and said earnestly: "I sure don't want no trouble with you, Ed. I expect you to marry her some day. I guess, if I had to pick out a man for her, I'd pick you, but, damn it, this ain't the time for her to leave home, so I want you to figger out some way to make her come back."

Ed sat motionless, still stunned, his eyes not leaving the M Bar man's face. He couldn't say anything. He simply did not believe what Wilson was saying, but he also knew that he was so shocked by Wilson's words that he wasn't thinking straight. The only coherent thought he had was that Wilson was up to something, but he had no idea what it was.

Wilson, unable to stand the silence, said impatiently: "Did you savvy what I told you?"

"Oh, I savvied, all right," Ed said, "but I'm going to have to think on it for a while. Your reason for Judy going back to the M Bar don't make much sense to me.

Seems like you wouldn't want her to be an old maid. If I'm the man you'd pick to marry her, looks like you'd want me to marry her while she of a notion to do it. She might pick a worse man."

Wilson nodded. "Yeah, she could, but I just don't think this is the right time. She's young. It won't hurt her to wait another year or two. I won't try to stop you, but if you are really thinking of her . . ."

"You won't stop us, and that's a fact," Ed said. "I think you made this whole thing up for some reason I ain't figured out yet."

Wilson grinned, a tight, humorless stretching of his lips against his teeth. "You don't know me very well, Ed. It's always been Curt you've dealt with. He's supposed to be Mister M Bar. Well, he ain't. *I am.* Have been ever since Curt lost his leg. But the point is, Judy is part of the M Bar. I can't even think of it without her being a part of it. Maybe I could in another year. That's why I want you to wait."

Ed rose and shook his head. "I won't wait. I couldn't get Judy to wait, either."

As he turned toward the batwings, Wilson demanded: "Where are you going?"

Ed stopped. "You've had your say, haven't you?"

"I've had my say about Judy," Wilson answered as he rose, a little uncertainly, Ed thought, as if the M Bar foreman didn't know where to go from here. "I've got some other things to say, but they'll wait. Right now, I want to talk to that gunslinger. I figured you might want to hear what he has to say. It'll tell you more about Pete Egan than anything Pete says to you."

Ed shrugged, not believing that any more than the other things Wilson had just told him. He'd never had much to do with the man. He'd been just another cowhand until Maulden had made him the M Bar ramrod a few years before, and it had only been after Maulden had lost his leg that Ed had heard much about Wilson. Now, looking at him, he thought Wilson had been right when he'd said Ed didn't know him. Maybe he was a devious, ambitious schemer, working toward some hidden goal that was not obvious to Ed and probably not to Judy, either.

"All right, I'll listen," Ed said, and left the saloon, Wilson keeping step with him as they walked to the hotel.

John Brown sat in his usual chair. Ed moved behind Wilson who stopped directly in front of Brown. He looked down on the gunman as he said: "I'm Curly Wilson. I run the M Bar south of town. Are you looking for a job?"

"No," Brown said.

"Would an offer of one hundred dollars a month and found change your mind?"

Brown took the cigar out of his mouth, his expressionless eyes on Wilson. "Ain't that a mite high for a riding job?"

"I'm hiring your guns," Wilson said. "I'm not asking you to take a thirty-a-month riding job."

"Expecting trouble?"

Wilson nodded. "It's been coming for a long time. I need a man like you."

"I ain't interested."

Wilson turned to face Ed. "See? It's just like I told you."

Wilson stepped past Ed and strode back to the Bull's Head where he had left his horse. He mounted and rode out of town. Ed dropped into a chair beside Brown. Neither spoke until Wilson was out of sight, then Brown said: "You know, Sheriff, it's downright interesting what a man can accomplish by just sitting."

"That's what I've thought ever since you got off the stage," Ed said.

"I sure didn't aim to kick up a cloud of dust," Brown said. "I've been on the go a long time. I just wanted to sit here and be let alone, but, by God, you'd think I was some kind of a freak out of Barnum's and Bailey's circus." He jerked a thumb in the direction Wilson had gone. "What was that all about?"

"I told you we had a range war building up," Ed said. "The M Bar belongs to Curt Maulden, but this Curly Wilson has been rodding the outfit. He thinks Pete Egan who has the Rafter E north of town hired you to fight for him."

"I ain't fighting for nobody," Brown said irritably. "I've had all the fighting I want."

"Now, on the other hand," Ed said, "Egan thinks Maulden hired you. That makes more sense, seeing as Egan already has a gunslinger on his payroll named Red Mike Kelso. I mentioned him to you."

"I remember," Brown nodded. "Well, if it'll help, tell both of 'em I ain't been hired by nobody."

"There's another thing that's damned funny," Ed said. "The banker, Sam Thorn, jumped me about running you out of town. Didn't give me no reason. I told him you hadn't given me any cause to do that. He got pretty huffy about it. Now, you tell me why he wants you out of town?"

"Is he a fat man?" Brown asked. "Dresses right fancy. Drives a new buggy and a bay mare?"

Ed nodded. "That's him."

"Never saw him before, but he walked past me this morning and then came driving by in his buggy a little later," Brown said. "Acted kind of funny. When he was walking, he looked straight ahead till he got about there." Brown pointed to a spot in front of him. "Then he sneaked a quick look at me and went on. I guessed he was a banker. They've got a way about 'em, like they're living off the fat of the land which same I guess they are." He shook his head. "But no, I don't have no idea why he wants me out of town."

"As near as I can guess," Ed said, "Thorn drove out to the Rafter E and talked to Kelso, gave him something which might have been money, so he's probably hired Kelso to kill you. I still don't know why, but chances are Kelso will show up this afternoon and promote a gun fight with you. I don't want that to happen."

"Damn it," Brown said, "I told you all I wanted was to just sit here. I won't have no part of a gun fight, if I can help it." He paused, his gaze pinned on Ed's face, then added: "But on the other hand, I ain't gonna jump up and hide to keep it from happening. If Kelso wants to die that bad, I'll oblige him."

108

"I savvy that," Ed said, "and I wouldn't expect you to do otherwise. I just want you to avoid it if you can." He shook his head. "I can figure Kelso. He's just a snot-nosed kid who's looking for trouble, but I can't figure Sam Thorn." He studied Brown's sun-burned face which had been devoid of expression even when his tone of voice had reflected his irritation. Then Ed said: "I still can't believe there isn't more to your being here than you're telling me. I want to know what it is."

"You've got to be satisfied with what I've told you," Brown said, "but I will say I ain't aiming to cause you no trouble. I've tangled enough with the law."

"That's fair enough," Ed said, and rose.

He remained motionless for a moment, staring down at the bleak-faced man. He believed what Brown said, and, for the first time since the gunman had come to Nugget City, he felt some sympathy for him. He had heard of men who had been caught in a net of circumstances, and through no fault on their part had been forced to run all their lives.

Perhaps that was true with this John Brown, but still there was his visit to Cathy Allen last night. Why had he gone at night to see her and why had he slipped in through her back door? He considered asking Brown about it, then decided against it. Brown was not a man to say anything he didn't want to say.

Without another word Ed swung away from the gunman toward the hotel door and went into the lobby.

Al Fleming stood behind the desk, anxious eyes on Ed. He asked in a low tone: "Learn anything, Sheriff?"

Ed shook his head as he approached the desk. "He's close-mouthed. He did turn down a job that Wilson offered him, which same don't mean anything. How about you?"

"Nothing," Fleming said. "He come into the dining room for breakfast. Pretty late. Almost nine, I think it was. Then he went back to his chair." The hotel man hesitated, worried eyes not leaving Ed's face. "I've been thinking about what you said, Sheriff. About Brown probably not being after me and all. I quit worrying for a while, but then, damn it, it all came back. I ain't gonna feel right till that jasper is dead or out of town."

"What makes you think he'll be dead?"

"Why, men like that always die young," Fleming answered.

"Maybe we've been misjudging him." Ed glanced at the clock on the wall back of Fleming. "Say, it's noon. I'd better get home for dinner."

He left the hotel, surprised that Fleming had started worrying about Brown's presence in town again, but probably it was the same with everyone else. Sam Thorn, at least, had not stopped worrying.

CHAPTER
FOURTEEN

Dinner was ready when Ed returned to the house. His mother called when he walked through the front door. "It's time you were getting home. Wash up."

Judy was nowhere in sight when Ed crossed the kitchen to the sink. He asked: "What'd you do with Judy? I told her not to leave the . . ."

"Hold your horses," his mother interrupted. "She ain't gone nowhere. She's upstairs sleeping. She went to bed right after you left. She's so tired she doesn't know what to do with herself. She didn't want to give up, but I made her go."

"You know you can't keep making your daughter-in-law do things," Ed said.

"I'll keep making her do things when she don't know what's good for her," Mrs McCoy snapped. "You know she didn't get any sleep last night to speak of. Poor lamb. I felt so sorry for her."

Ed sat down and began to eat, knowing there was no use pursuing the conversation. She had "mothered" his father until Fist would walk out of the house, muttering that women ought to have kids to look after till they were ninety. Ed had often felt the same way after he was grown, and he knew it would not be different until

111

he had moved into a house of his own. He wasn't even sure that he'd be free then of his mother's domination, and he had a feeling it would be worse for Judy.

He didn't mention his talk with Curly Wilson until they had finished eating. He hadn't made up his mind whether he would tell her or not until she asked: "What did Wilson want with you?"

He leaned back in his chair, stirring his coffee. He decided then to tell her because she had often talked to Mrs Maulden and therefore might know something about Judy's parentage, although he doubted that Judy's mother would ever have mentioned her moment of indiscretion.

"You won't believe it," Ed said, "but he claims Curt is not Judy's father."

"Hogwash." Mrs McCoy laughed shortly. "Of course, he is. She even looks like him."

Ed didn't believe that was true, but he let it go. He said: "Wilson claims Curt couldn't have children."

"Rubbish," Mrs McCoy snapped. "There was nothing wrong with Curt. It was Judy's mother. She was always kind of delicate, and she had a hard time giving birth to Judy. After that, old Doc Curry said she would never have another child, and it grieved both Curt and her something fierce. They wanted a houseful of kids."

She rose and, going to the stove, picked up the coffee pot and filled their cups. She returned to the table and sat down, then suddenly straightened her back and stared at Ed. "Just who does Mister Smart Alec Wilson think was Judy's father?"

"He says he was," Ed said.

For a moment he was tempted to laugh when he saw the amazed expression on his mother's face. She froze, her coffee cup half way to her mouth, her eyes wide, her lips parted. Slowly she set the cup on the table and shouted: "Now that really is hogwash. Just how did he manage to get into the Maulden bed? I suppose Curt moved over for him?"

He told her what Curly Wilson had said. She nodded and admitted that the part about flowers and the yard and the garden was true, that Wilson had been about Mrs Maulden's age, and they could have been alone on the M Bar for a few days, but then she shook her head.

"I knew that girl well," she said. "She was a good young woman who would never under any condition have broken her marriage vows. Wilson was right in saying she was not happy living with Curt Maulden, and I know damn' well he abused her, although how Pete Egan ever found out about it I never knew. Just guessed, maybe, knowing Maulden as well as he did."

"I figured that," Ed agreed, "but then I couldn't see why Curly told me about it. He claimed he'd kill me if I ever told anyone else."

"You told me," Mrs McCoy said. "Now I guess he'll have to kill you."

Ed shrugged. "I told you because I thought there was a slim chance that Judy's mother might have said something that would give you an angle on it."

"Nothing that would bear out Wilson's crazy notion." She lifted the coffee cup to her lips, and this time took a long drink before she set the cup down. "As

113

to why Wilson would tell you, well, I think we don't know Wilson very well."

"That's right," Ed agreed. "He was the sort of man you'd never notice in a crowd of cowboys, even after Curt made him foreman, but later, after Curt lost his leg, Wilson began to change. He'd talk a little louder in a saloon on Saturday night. He'd get proddy after he had a few drinks. He just seemed to want to be noticed. From what Judy says, he runs the M Bar the way he wants to." He shook his head. "But that don't answer our question."

"Suppose," Mrs McCoy said thoughtfully, "he really does want Judy back home, and he thinks it would break up your marriage if he told you?"

"Why would it do that?"

"It would make Judy illegitimate. Some men wouldn't want to marry a bastard."

"Oh hell . . . ," he began and paused, another thought flashing across his mind. "He said that Curt used to be Mister M Bar, but now he was. Maybe he wants the M Bar himself when Curt dies which might be any time."

"And Judy would turn to him to run the outfit," Mrs McCoy said. "Maybe even marry her some day, if he could keep you from marrying her now."

Ed nodded. "Looks to me like he's a scheming son of a bitch. I guess it goes to prove that you can know a man for years and still not know him at all." He rose. "How long do you figure Judy will sleep?"

"I dunno," Mrs McCoy answered. "I'll have to wake her pretty soon or she won't sleep tonight."

114

"I'm riding out to the M Bar this afternoon," Ed said, "and I want to ask her a couple of questions before I do."

His mother shook her head at him. "I don't think that's very smart, Ed. You're not going to find out anything from Curt Maulden. Like Judy said, he'll blow your head off before you get a chance to say a word."

"Maybe not," Ed said. "Anyhow, it's something I've got to do. If I didn't, and Maulden and Egan started shooting, I'd always figure I should have done more to stop it." He walked to the living room door, then paused to say: "I've got one chore to do before I leave town. I'll stop and see Judy before I leave."

"You ain't gonna tell Judy what Wilson said, are you?" Mrs McCoy demanded.

"Hell no," Ed said. "Don't you open your mouth about it, either. Judy'll be happier if she never knows."

Mrs McCoy nodded. "She's got enough to worry about. She may think she hates her pa, but she feels guilty about leaving home just the same."

Ed left the house and walked rapidly to Cathy Allen's place on Main Street. This again was an attempt to find the truth that Ed did not think would tell him anything, but like the other efforts he knew he had to try.

Cathy opened the door to his knock. When he looked at her, he thought she was an uncommonly pretty girl, the same thought he always had when he saw her, but now the additional thought crossed his mind that she deserved a better man than the gunfighter, Brown.

Ed touched the brim of his hat as he said: "Howdy, Cathy."

Her face showed surprise when she saw who her caller was, then she backed up a step and started to shut the door in his face. She had plainly panicked. He didn't know her well, but she had always seemed to him to be a courageous and self-possessed young woman. Now he was shocked to see the terror that so obviously possessed her.

Cathy recovered quickly and said in a friendly tone: "Good afternoon, Sheriff. Have I broken the law?"

"Not that I know of," Ed answered. "I have a question I'd like to ask."

She hesitated, her eyes searching his face. Fear was still there, and she seemed very uncertain, but finally she said: "Come in. We'll go back to the kitchen. I don't suppose you'd feel at ease in a room like this." She indicated the sewing machine, the clothes dummy, and the cutting table with a wave of her hand. "I've had to turn my living room into a work room."

He nodded to show he understood and followed her on through the clutter to her kitchen. She motioned for him to sit down at the table as she asked: "I just put a fresh pot of coffee on the stove. Will you have a cup?"

He shook his head. "Thanks, but I just got up from having dinner."

She sat down across from him and placed her hands on top of the table. "I'll answer any question I can, unless I have to incriminate myself."

He hesitated, wondering if the question *would* incriminate her. She had an open, honest face that made most people like her as soon as they met her. Those who didn't were probably jealous of her beauty,

Ed thought. Still, he couldn't remember ever hearing anyone criticize her about anything, and, from what his mother had said, she had all the work she wanted.

"As I'm sure you know," Ed said, "we have a stranger in town who has stirred up quite a commotion."

"I know."

"You may think this is none of my business," he went on, "and maybe it isn't, but I hope you'll answer my question, because we're sitting on a powder keg that may blow up in our faces at any time. I'm trying to keep that from happening. My question is how much do you know about this man who calls himself John Brown?"

Cathy's face turned pale. She rose and, going to the stove, poured herself a cup of coffee and returned to the table, then asked: "Why?"

"Because he's scared some people just by showing up here," Ed answered. "As far as I know, he is not wanted by the law. Leastwise I don't have a reward dodger on him, but he don't act right. He's got me boogered because he may touch off a powder keg without meaning to."

"What makes you think I know anything about him?"

"Because, when I was making my rounds last night, I saw him go into your house," Ed answered. "You let him in through the back door, so you must know him."

She took a long breath, her head lowered as she studied her cup of coffee. Finally she said: "This is none of your business, and it has nothing to do with your powder keg, but I'll tell you anyway. He's the man

117

I'm going to marry. He came here to see me. We'll be leaving soon, I think. I assure you he did not expect all the attention he has received and didn't want it."

"I don't understand why he has to come to see you after dark and go in through your back door."

"We just didn't want to attract any attention," she said. "I guess we went at it the wrong way."

"I'm afraid you did," Ed said. "In fact, it attracted more attention than if he had just gone about his business. I still don't understand his actions. Or yours, either. No one would have thought anything about it, if he called on you as I would expect a fiancé to do."

She sipped her coffee, her eyes still on him. "I'm sorry, Sheriff. That's all I can tell you. Like I said, we did it the wrong way, and I'm sorry we caused you so much concern."

He rose, hesitated as he looked down at her, but she had her feelings under control now, and he could tell nothing from her expression. Color had returned to her cheeks, and, if she were still frightened, she did not show it.

"I'll leave you with your work," he said, "but I'm still not satisfied. Maybe it's just a hunch, but it doesn't make much sense for a gunslinger to come to Nugget City to see his girl and then spend his time sitting in front of the hotel. If you decide to tell me anything more, you can find me at home or in my office. I will be gone for three or four hours this afternoon, but I'll be in town after that."

He left the room. She followed him across the kitchen and across the work room, opened the door for him, then said: "Good afternoon, Sheriff." She closed the door behind him.

As he walked back to his house, he realized that she had told him only a small part of what he wanted to know. John Brown and Cathy Allen were up to something, and it had to be criminal, or at least illegal. Otherwise Cathy would have given him the whole story, and he felt certain somehow that she hadn't.

CHAPTER
FIFTEEN

When Ed returned home, he found Judy sitting at the table, nibbling at her dinner. He bent down and kissed her, and she reached up and hugged him. When he stepped back and looked down at her, he thought she looked more tired than when he had seen her that morning. He sat down beside her, and she took his hand.

"I look a fright," she said. "I wish you'd come in five minutes from now. I just got up. I'm not one bit hungry, but your mother made me sit down and try to eat."

He laughed. "She's always making someone do something. You surely remember how it was when you lived here before. It's just something you'll have to put up with until we're married and have our own house."

"Oh, I don't mind," Judy said. "She was probably right about me eating. She said it was too long to wait for supper." She sighed. "I guess I would have slept till dark, but then I wouldn't sleep tonight if I hadn't got up."

"You're not used to having a woman tell you what to do any more," he said. "I suppose Curt let you run the house."

She nodded. "The only time we had any trouble was when Curly wanted me to help with the cattle, and Pa said I had my own work to do. Well, I did, but I liked to get out of the house once in a while." She squeezed his hand. "I guess that won't be any problem after we're married."

"No, I reckon not," he agreed.

"You know," she said thoughtfully. "I've lived so long with men that I may have trouble in town. I'll be with women a lot more."

"Oh, you'll get used to it." He grinned, then his face turned grave. "Judy, there's a couple of questions I want to ask you. I'm riding up the creek to the M Bar this afternoon. You said Curt would blow my head off if I showed up there, but I've got to find a way to talk to him."

She stared at him questioningly. "You've got to go?"

He nodded. "I've been grabbing at straws, just trying to figure out what's happened since that damned gunman came to town. I still am."

She was silent for a time, her head lowered, her eyes on her plate. Finally she said: "I'd hate to have you try to talk to Pa. I don't know what he'll do. It's like trying to figure out which way the wind's going to blow. He's rational most of the time and can be very polite, then you mention Pete Egan or anything that makes him mad, and he blows up. He can change in a second. Sometimes you don't even know what you said that did it."

"I'll be careful in what I say."

She raised her head to look at him, her forehead creased in worry. "I don't know, Ed. I just don't know. He may try to kill you. No matter how careful you are with what you say, you may set him off. He has always been hard to live with, but he's been worse since he lost his leg. He just sits there on the front porch in any kind of weather and broods about his leg, or losing the M Bar, or Curly. He doesn't trust Curly. He thinks Curly's robbing him."

"Is he?"

"Of course not. Pa just doesn't trust anybody."

"How about the other question," Ed said. "I want you to think hard. How has Curly treated you?"

She hesitated, questioning eyes on him. "What makes you ask?"

"I'm beginning to wonder about him," Ed said. "Mostly since he was here this morning. I've always liked him. Thought he was honest. Smart. Decent. Now I don't know. Sometimes men appear to be good men and still can be downright ornery. My father used to say never trust a man because he acts and looks law abiding. I guess Sam Thorn is like that, though he's easier to see through than most men."

"Curly helped raise me," Judy said. "I guess I'd trust him with my life."

"I know," Ed nodded. "But that doesn't really answer my question. What kind of a man is he inside?"

"When I was little, he'd come to the house in the evenings and play with me. When I got older, he taught me all I know about horses and riding and how to help out on roundup. He'd take me fishing." She paused and

122

sat reflecting about it for a time, then she went on. "I never really thought about it before. I just took Curly for granted, like he was part of the family. Pa never paid any attention to him. I mean, his being with me so much. I suppose he was glad to get me off his hands, but some of the housekeepers were upset about it and wouldn't let me leave the house with Curly to go fishing or anything. They never told me why."

"Was it like that after you finished high school and went back home?"

"No, it was different. I guess it was kind of hard for him to realize I had finally grown up and was a woman. I'd been more boy than girl before, I guess. I got so I was a little reluctant to be with him alone, and I don't really know why. He still liked to hug me and pat me on the back the way he always had. Just being affectionate. After you and I were engaged, I didn't like to have him touch me."

Ed thought about what she had said, silent for a moment. It was possible that Curly was her father and wanted to help raise her and spend as much time with her as possible. On the other hand, it could be that he thought of her in a different way, and that could be the reason he was unable to bear the thought of her marrying another man.

"I've heard that you look a lot like your mother," Ed said.

She nodded. "I don't know what that's got to do with it, but people have told me that. It's a compliment, I guess. She must have been a very beautiful woman."

"Is Curly more anxious to have you come back than your pa?" Ed asked.

"Oh, yes." She grimaced and went on. "That sounds kind of queer, doesn't it? Pa never says he likes me, or thanks me for anything I do. Maybe he doesn't know how to, but I don't think he really cares one way or the other except that I save him money when I'm there to do the housework.

"He never worried about me marrying you, except how it will probably make him have to hire a housekeeper, but Curly was upset from the day I announced we were engaged. He was really angry. He talked about how much I owed Pa, and it wasn't right for me to leave home, with Pa's leg gone and all. I never thought much about it then. I just expected Curly to feel that way." Suddenly she rose and began walking nervously around the room, her face reflecting her worry. Suddenly she whirled to face Ed. "You're getting at something. What is it?"

"I think we've been taken in by Curly," Ed said. "Maybe Curt's right not to trust him, and it makes me wonder why he doesn't fire Curly."

"He trusted Curly before his accident," Judy said. "Now he doesn't know what to do. There's nobody else in the crew who could ramrod the M Bar. Anyhow, Pa has a hard time making any decision. That's what surprised me when Pa told Curly to finish the dam. I can't remember when he's said anything so definite as that."

Ed rose, kissed Judy, then held her for several seconds before he said: "I'll be back sometime this afternoon. Don't worry about me."

124

"Oh, no," she said, smiling. "I won't worry about you one little bit."

"Good," he said, and left the house.

He mounted and rode along Main Street until he reached the hotel, then he reined up in front of John Brown. "Any sign of Red Mike Kelso?" he asked.

Brown shook his head. "I think you're trying to scare me out of town," he said. "If that's your game, forget it."

"I ain't trying to scare you into anything," Ed said irritably. "He'll show up," and rode out of town on the M Bar road.

The widest and best part of the valley lay south of town. This was where the farmers and small ranchers lived, land that was mortgaged to Sam Thorn and in time would probably be taken over by the bank. Logically this part of the valley could not be claimed by either Pete Egan or Curt Maulden, and probably neither wanted it because they both needed the hay the farmers produced.

Egan had another angle which profited him. None of the small outfits had enough cattle to afford a drive to Gunnison, so they sold their steers to Egan who threw them in with his herd each fall. Naturally he did not pay the going price in Gunnison, so there was always some grumbling among the ten-cow ranchers who felt they were being taken advantage of. Ed had heard some of them talk of forming a pool herd and making their own drives, but they always wound up following their old pattern of selling to Egan.

Ed thought they were afraid of Egan, but he also knew they were small-thinking men with no leader among them, so their knuckling under may have been more a lack of leadership than fear. As Ed followed the county road that ran between the hay fields, the grass almost tall enough to cut, he thought about Egan's ambition to own the M Bar and told himself it was ridiculous. The ranches were too far apart to be run as one operation.

As Ed turned it over in his mind, he decided that Egan was not thinking about how good the investment would be. Probably his only consideration was his desire to take something that belonged to Curt Maulden.

Foolish as it seemed, their mutual hatred was the guiding motive in both men's lives. Ed had been too young to remember the beginning of the feud, but, if his mother was right, it went back to the time Maulden married Judy's mother, and it would probably go on as long as both men were alive. In the end, Ed thought sourly, Sam Thorn would end up owning both spreads along with the rest of the valley.

Five miles above Nugget City the hills on both sides of the valley closed in to become high cliffs. The cañon that the road followed to the M Bar had been cut by the creek which pounded noisily downcañon to Ed's left. So the dam hadn't been finished, but Ed was doubtful if he could get it stopped in time to prevent a showdown.

Half an hour later he emerged from the narrow cañon into the valley that was the core of the M Bar. It was a mile or more wide and several miles long, one of the many mountain parks that were common in the Colorado Rockies.

The grass here was always at least two weeks behind the lower valley grass and would not be as tall. The soil was more shallow, the climate more severe, and therefore the M Bar would never be as prosperous as the Rafter E. Maulden could not run as many cattle as Egan did or hire as big a crew, so, if it came to a showdown, Egan held the winning hand.

Snow-capped peaks surrounded the M Bar, the foothills covered by aspens with dark fingers of spruce running down to the level floor of the valley. For some reason Ed was always reminded of a huge cake when he was here, the cake surrounded by a great circle of white icing. The sheer beauty of the park that now lay in front of him always was breath-taking, but he wondered if Maulden saw any beauty in it. Probably not. He had looked at it too long.

Ahead of Ed was a small mesa, the M Bar corrals and buildings on top, a cluster of aspens adding a splash of green leaves and white trunks. It was the only touch of beauty about the place. The house was log, squat and graceless, built only for utility. Neither Maulden's wife nor Judy had been able to do much to change its basic ugliness.

Ed reached the barbed-wire fence that ran east and west across the valley just below the mesa. The gate was padlocked as he expected, so he stepped down and tied his horse to a fence post. As he turned toward the house, Curt Maulden's harsh voice knifed at him: "Stop right there, or I'll blow your goddamned head off."

CHAPTER
SIXTEEN

Cathy Allen was trembling when she closed the door behind Ed McCoy. She had not expected a visit from him, so she had been utterly unprepared for it and his questions, and now she felt she had handled the situation badly. But what could she have said? She had not wanted her connection with John Brown to become common knowledge until after she had received the blackmail money from Sam Thorn, but she'd never dreamed that the sheriff would be cruising around her back door after dark. John might just as well have come in through the front door and left the same way.

She returned to the kitchen and poured another cup of coffee. She sat down at the table and began to think about her situation. Her nerves soon quieted, and she was no longer quivering like an aspen leaf. It probably didn't make any difference, she thought, that McCoy knew John was her lover.

The sheriff had no way of knowing about their blackmailing scheme, so he couldn't do anything to stop them. They'd buy two horses and, as soon as they got their money, they'd be out of town. McCoy probably would never know what had happened. Thorn wouldn't tell, even to get his $5,000 back.

Still Cathy could not shake off her uneasiness. For the first time she began to doubt the plan that she had dreamed about for so long. Maybe it never had been practical. Maybe Thorn had not sent to Gunnison for his money. Maybe he had never intended to do it. Maybe her idea of having John come and sit in front of the hotel, wearing his two guns, had not been a guarantee that Thorn would be scared into paying the blackmail money. Perhaps they would have been better off to have played it straight, with her going directly to Thorn and John right there beside her. She'd been too obvious, and it just wasn't going to work.

She paced back and forth in the kitchen, sick at her stomach as the waves of doubt assaulted her. John had not been impressed by her plan, but he'd gone along with her because it was the way she wanted it. Now, if Thorn didn't keep his bargain, John would take it out on him in one way or the other. He'd never have come to Nugget City if she hadn't built up her sure-fire scheme in her letters to him.

She stopped pacing, thinking she heard the stage coming. She ran though her work room to the front door and opened it just as the coach wheeled past with its usual jangle of trace chains and whip cracking and whirling dust. She stayed inside until the dust settled, then stepped through the front door to the porch.

The stage pulled up in front of the hotel, the driver stepped down, opened the door, and helped a woman to the ground. At this distance she couldn't recognize the woman, but it didn't make any difference who she was. What was important, and what she hoped to see,

129

was Thorn's leaving the bank to go to the stage and receiving the packet of money that should have arrived.

Her hopes died when the driver climbed up to the high seat and drove away. Thorn had not made his appearance. She stood motionless for a few minutes, wondering what she should do now. The last thing she wanted to do was to go to the hotel and tell John that their plan had failed, that Thorn had simply ignored the threats she had made.

Well, she'd go to Thorn first. Maybe he'd take the money from the cash he had in the bank safe. She didn't believe it, but it was the one hope to which she could cling. She wanted to leave town without any trouble; she did not want John to tangle with Ed McCoy. She did not doubt how a gun fight would come out, but killing the sheriff was not part of her plans and would only result in trouble for them. Besides, she liked and respected McCoy. If John shot or beat up Thorn, the sheriff would have to make a move.

She had to know. There was no reason to wait and keep on torturing herself, so she left the house and walked rapidly to the corner, crossed to the bank side of the street, and reached it without glancing at John. He probably was having the same thoughts she was, but was waiting to hear from her.

When Cathy crossed the lobby to the door of Thorn's office, the cashier rose and ran toward her, shouting: "Miss Allen, I have strict orders not to let you or anyone else in to see Mister Thorn today."

She stopped, one hand on the door knob. She said: "Morgan, I don't give a damn what your orders are.

130

This is a matter of life and death, and I am going to see Thorn now. If you stop me, it will be a question of life and death for you as well as Thorn."

He stared at her blankly, but apparently her tone of voice and the expression on her face frightened him. He backed away, shaking his head in bewilderment. He was neither a brave nor intelligent man, she thought, but who could be brave working for Sam Thorn, and certainly no one with intelligence would have put up with Thorn's greedy and domineering ways as long as Morgan had.

Cathy turned the knob and opened the door. Thorn was standing at the window. There was a vacant lot next to the bank, so he had an angled view of the street. He was so intent on what he was seeing, or expected to see, that he was not aware of her presence until she said: "Thorn, I'm here for the money you sent to Gunnison for."

He wheeled, surprised, and stood motionless, staring blankly at her as if it took a moment for him to grasp what she was talking about. His face paled, and, as he turned from the window to move to his desk, Cathy saw that he walked in the tottery manner of an old man.

He sat down and rubbed his face with his hands, then he said: "Miss Allen, I did not send for any money. There is no one in Gunnison I could get that much money from on such short notice. I can't spare it from the capital I have in my safe. I simply will not let my bank be bankrupted by a scheming woman who tries to blackmail me, so you might as well leave."

131

This was what she had expected to hear. Still, she had hoped it would not be this way. She didn't move for a moment, her eyes on the banker. He was not looking at her. Instead, he was staring at his desk, a muscle in his right cheek beating with the regularity of a pulse.

"You are willing to have me spread the truth about you and Sally York around town?" she asked finally.

"No, I'm not willing," he answered. "For your own sake I hope you won't, but I can't stop you if you're determined to do it. I told you I can't spare the money."

"But you own more than half the town," she said.

"That's not cash," he said wearily. "I'm property poor. It doesn't help in this situation to own property."

"You know my friend will be calling on you," she warned him.

"I can't stop him from coming," he said.

"You made a bargain," she cried.

A hint of a smile touched his lips. "You are, I'm afraid, a very naïve young woman. Now will you leave?"

Still she stood there, her gaze not leaving his face. Either he had decided to let the gossip about him and Sally York be known to everybody in Nugget City, or he had some other object in mind. That was it, she decided, but what?

"You're making a mistake, Thorn," she said. "You don't know my friend."

She left then, realizing that Thorn was walking back to the window. She left the bank, her heart hammering. She hesitated when she was outside, the afternoon sun

132

throwing her long shadow across the board walk. Brown was looking at her, so she crossed the street to him, knowing she might as well get it over with.

As she sat down beside him, he said: "From the look on your face, your sneaky little scheme didn't pan out."

"No," she admitted. "I guess I wanted to get out of this stinking little town and away from the ungrateful women I work for, and wanted to be with you and have something of our own . . ." Her voice trailed off.

"You got carried away by your dreaming," he said. "That it?"

"That's it," she said.

He shrugged. "I didn't think much of your scheme in the first place, but I figured you had to give it a try. Well, there's always men who'll hire my guns."

"No," she said, her jaw set stubbornly. "I'm not giving up yet. I want you to visit Thorn. He's got the money right there in the bank. I'm sure of it. If we scare him enough, he'll find it."

"Well, I can throw the fear of God into him," Brown said, "but I ain't sure it's a good idea. It's my guess he's decided to bull it through and let you do your worst."

"I don't think so," Cathy said. "He's got some scheme to best us. I don't know what it is, but he's thought of something."

"I can tell you what it is," Brown said, "if the sheriff knows what he's talking about. Thorn's hired a gunslinger named Red Mike Kelso to kill me."

Her heart missed a beat, then began to race as fear washed through her. She had hoped to avoid violence. This had seemed so easy when she'd first thought of it.

133

Thorn had struck her as a fat blob of jelly who was tough only when he had somebody else whipsawed. Hiring Kelso was the last thing she would have thought of his doing.

Cathy's hand went out to grip him. "What do we do?" she whispered. "I don't want you having a gun fight with Kelso."

His face showed no worry. If anything, the slight smile on his thin lips cut some of the usual grimness from his face. Sometimes, she thought, he actually welcomed the danger that he had faced for so many years, the danger she had wanted to remove from his life.

"I ain't asking for no fight," he said, "but, if it comes to that, I ain't duckin' it. That's the way I've always lived, and the way I've got to live."

"If you are killed," she said miserably, "there would be nothing for me to live for. I might as well have him kill me, too. It's not worth it, John."

"Quit worrying," he said sharply. "I don't aim to get killed. I've seen his kind before, kids hell-bent on making a reputation for themselves. The bigger the reputation, the more they can hire their gun out for. I'll try to talk him out of it, but most of 'em are so cock sure they're good that they're willing to die, trying to prove it."

"Suppose he *is* that good?"

"He ain't," Brown answered. "They never are. They come up like weeds in a garden and die, and more come along. It ain't none of my doing."

"That's not what worries me," she said. "You know the old saying about there never was a horse that couldn't be rode or a man who couldn't . . ."

"Sure, sure," he said impatiently. "I can't afford to let it apply to me, so shut up about it." He paused, then added: "Why did you come over here and sit down beside me? Now everybody will know about us."

"It doesn't make any difference," she said. "I just wanted you to do it that way because I thought your being here would scare Thorn, but it didn't scare him enough."

"It seems I scared a lot of other people," he said dryly. "Now about calling on your friend Thorn. We'll wait till after Kelso shows up. Thorn just might change his mind after he sees Kelso lying in the street. Right now, he wouldn't pay any attention because he's counting on Kelso's salivating me."

He glanced along the street and straightened up, then nodded at a rider moving toward them from the north. "You know Kelso?" he asked.

"I know him by sight," she said. "I've never talked to him."

"That him?"

She didn't want to look; she didn't even want to admit that a man named Red Mike Kelso existed, but she made herself turn her head to look at the approaching rider. She didn't answer until the man had dismounted and tied in front of the Bull's Head, then she breathed, "That's him."

CHAPTER
SEVENTEEN

Ed stood motionless beside the M Bar gate, knowing he was very close to death, that the wrong move or wrong word would bring a bullet. At this distance Curt Maulden was not likely to miss, so Ed didn't move a muscle as he called: "How are you, Curt?" Maulden was standing on the porch, his rifle raised to his shoulder. For a moment he didn't move or say anything, then Ed shouted: "I'm Ed McCoy. I came out to visit you."

Maulden lowered his rifle as he called: "McCoy! You the sheriff?"

"That's right," Ed answered. "I rode out from town just to see how you are."

"McCoy," Maulden repeated. "Why, I ain't seen you for a coon's age. Come on up."

Ed slipped between two strands of barbed wire and walked up the slope to the house. Maulden had backed up and sat down in a rocking chair, his Winchester across his lap. Ed had not been here for a long time, a year or more, and the place looked seedier than ever. Judy had tried to plant some flowers and a few hardy vegetables in a garden east of the house, but she'd never had any help, so she had given up because she simply didn't have the time or strength to do everything that she wanted and needed to do.

Maulden had built his log house when he'd first taken up the land and had never added to it or changed it. The outbuildings were the same, built of logs, weathered by the elements, and all needed repair. Trash was scattered around the place, old bits of metal and lumber and various odds and ends that no one had bothered to pick up for years.

As Ed climbed the steps to the porch, he wondered, as he always had when he'd come out to see Judy, how she could have lived here as long as she had. He knew it had been difficult for her, and he promised himself that, after they were married, her life would be different.

Ed extended his hand as he said: "I'm glad to see you again, Curt. You're looking fine."

It was a lie because Curt Maulden looked terrible. He was about Pete Egan's age, somewhere in his middle fifties, but he seemed twenty years older. He was very thin, his crêpe-like skin pulled tightly across the bones of his face. As they shook hands, Ed saw that his fingers were more like talons than fingers, and the backs of his hands were covered with dark splotches. His fever-bright eyes bored into Ed's face as he stared at him, apparently trying to recognize him and finding no resemblance to the man he had expected to see.

"You ain't the sheriff," Maulden said. "Why, he was a man my age, and you ain't no older'n an oversized pup."

"That was Fist McCoy you're thinking about," Ed said. "He was my father. He died a year or so ago, and I was appointed sheriff to take his place."

"Oh, hell, yes," Maulden said. "I remember now. You're the young squirt who used to ride out here, chasing Judy. She left home you know. Left last night without saying a damn' word to nobody. I suppose she went to see you."

Ed nodded. "She's staying at our place. My mother will look after her."

"She's a good girl," Maulden said. "Kind of a headstrong filly, but she works hard. Gonna be tough getting along without her. Always cooked my meals the way I liked 'em and kept house for me real good. I don't blame her for leaving, though. It was lonesome for her around here, you know."

He motioned to a captain's chair a few feet from his rocker. "Sit down, bub. You look a lot like your pa. I remember old Fist well. A good lawman when this country was wilder'n a wolf on the prowl."

Ed sat down as Maulden pulled a blackened briar from his shirt pocket and dribbled pipe tobacco into the bowl. Ed was surprised that he had found Curt Maulden reasonably sane and coherent. He was surprised, too, that Maulden was not in a rage over Judy's having left the ranch. He might be a minute from now, but for the moment at least he was temperate and friendly.

"I thought you'd be worried about Judy," Ed said, "so I wanted to tell you she's well and safe at our house. My mother was always very fond of her. You'll

138

remember she stayed with us when she was going to high school."

Maulden nodded as he struck a match and fired his pipe. "I recollect that. Said your ma was a good cook, and she learned a lot just staying there. Her ma died when she was little, and all of them damned housekeepers I hired didn't teach her nothing." He took the pipe from his mouth and jabbed the stem at Ed. "You fixing to marry her?"

"Yes," Ed said, wondering how that knowledge would affect Maulden. "In a few days, I think. I don't believe she's picked a day yet."

"Good," Maulden nodded in satisfaction. "You take care of her, boy. You hear me? You take care of her good, or I'll come after you with a blacksnake."

"You won't need it," Ed said. "I'll take good care of her. Oh, I was wondering if you knew Curly Wilson rode into town this morning and tried to get her to come back. Said you were real upset about her leaving and you needed her."

Maulden pulled on his pipe, apparently untouched by Ed's words. "Well, Curly's a damn' fool. You know, he's always been kind of loco about Judy. He was the same about her ma when she was alive. Acted like he was her brother. I married her when she was just a girl, and Curly wasn't more'n a whippersnapper when I hired him. I taught him everything he knows, and now he thinks he knows more'n I do."

Ed hesitated, not certain whether Maulden could handle what he wanted to tell him or not, but he decided it was the time to try. He said casually: "Curly bought me a drink in the Bull's Head and promised he'd kill me if I told anyone, but he claims he's Judy's father."

Nothing happened. Maulden kept on puffing for a moment, then he cried: "I'm getting tired of hearing Curly's lies. I wish I could fire him, but I can't run the outfit no more, and I don't know who I'd get if I let him go."

Ed was silent a moment, thinking that Maulden had not mentioned hitting Judy. Maybe he had forgotten he had done it. He still appeared normal, but Ed couldn't forget that the wrong word might set him off. Ed had been afraid that telling him what Wilson had said would do it, but he hadn't been upset by that, so maybe he had better control of himself than Ed thought.

"I don't savvy this," Ed said finally. "Why would Curly claim to be Judy's father?"

"Well, I don't know," Maulden said. "Only thing I do know is that my wife wouldn't have let him get within ten feet of her bed. He wanted to, all right. Wasn't no brotherly feeling about that. He just never got what he wanted from her."

Ed found it hard to decide what was the truth and what were lies, but he was inclined to believe Maulden's version which was close to what his mother had said. Still, there was something missing.

"I still don't savvy what Curly was up to," Ed said. "Him saying you wanted Judy back so bad and all."

"Chances are he told you that, hoping you'd feel sorry for him and you'd send her home." He puffed a moment, then went on. "I've been some worried about her 'cause I don't trust Curly. He's been waiting a long time for her to grow up. He'll go loco if you marry her. He'll try to kill you, figgering that if you was out of his way, she'd marry him."

Ed sat, staring across the valley, suddenly feeling tension gathering in Maulden's sick brain. The thought came to Ed that Maulden was trying to use him to get rid of Wilson.

"You hear me?" Maulden demanded, raising his voice. "Damn it, I'm warning you. I've knowed for a long time that Curly Wilson wasn't the man we all thought he was. He changed after I lost my leg. I think he's robbing me blind, but I can't get out and prove what I think. That's why I'm glad Judy left home."

Ed hesitated, realizing that the conversation had become very tricky. Maulden still seemed sane, but anger was building in him, and that could turn him into a crazy man in a second.

"I'm hearing you, all right," Ed said, knowing he had to pretend he was in complete agreement with Maulden. "I was just worrying about Judy while you were talking. I'm not sure what Curly will try to do."

"You've gotta keep your eyes on him," Maulden said. "That's all."

"There's another queer thing that's happened," Ed said. "We had a gunslick come to town who's worrying all of us. He hasn't done anything except sit in front of the hotel, but folks don't know why he came to town or what he's up to. Curly offered him a job. Wanted to hire his guns and promised him one hundred dollars a month."

Maulden snorted. "That was his idea, not mine. If he'd taken the job, I'd have sent him packing. The last thing we need is a gunslinger."

"That's what I thought," Ed said, "so I was surprised when Curly made the offer."

He rose, his gaze on the upper end of the valley where he could see men working on the dam, but from here he could not see how much had been done, so he had no idea when it would be finished. He hesitated, still not having said what he had come here to say. Now he was afraid to say it, sensing that Maulden's sanity was ebbing rapidly.

"Glad you came out," Maulden said, his voice still friendly. "I won't worry no more about Judy. She's your girl now."

"I'll make her happy," Ed promised.

He took one step to leave, then decided he had to chance Maulden's ability to discuss the dam problem rationally. He said: "Curt, Judy told me you're aiming to finish the dam and cut Egan's water off, but legally you can't . . ."

Maulden released his grip on the railing and thumbed back the hammer of his Winchester as he brought the barrel into line with Ed's chest, but he moved slowly and uncertainly, wobbling on his one good leg and his wooden one. Ed reached out, grabbed the barrel of the rifle, and twisted it out of Maulden's hands.

"Sit down before you fall down, Curt," Ed said. "You're dead wrong about why I came out here. I'm just trying to avoid a range war and men getting killed."

142

But now there was no trace of sanity in Maulden. He dropped into his rocking chair, his face distorted with the insane rage that gripped him. He picked up his crutch and swung the end at Ed's head, cursing and screaming wild threats. Ed backed away, the crutch missing him narrowly.

"I'll leave your Winchester down at the gate," Ed said. "You'd better think about one thing before you finish that dam. If you turn Egan's water off, I'll have to jail you. It is *his* water, you know."

He left on the run, certain that Maulden would still try to kill him. In one second the rancher had changed from a reasonable man into a maniacal killer. Ed glanced back once to see Maulden, hobbling into the house. He reached the fence, crawled through it, and untied his horse. As he swung into the saddle, he saw that Maulden was back on the porch, another rifle in his hands.

Ed dug steel into his horse's flanks as he heard the first crack of Maulden's rifle. He bent low in the saddle, bullets digging up little geysers of dust on one side of him and then the other, none coming close. It was not until he was out of sight in the cañon below the M Bar that he reined his horse down to a walk.

He rode slowly then, trying to sort out in his mind what Maulden had said. Again, it was a question of what were lies and what was the truth, but it seemed to Ed that Maulden had been entirely rational until the dam was mentioned, so everything he had said about Curly Wilson was probably true.

In any case, Ed was certain of one thing. Judy had left home barely in time. He was not sure what would have happened to her if she had stayed, but, whatever it was, it would not happen now. A feeling of relief followed him all the way to town, but the relief was diluted by doubt. What would Curly Wilson do?

CHAPTER
EIGHTEEN

Cathy Allen sat motionless, her hands clenched into tight little fists, her eyes glued on the approaching Kelso. Waves of guilt washed through her. She was responsible for this. If she hadn't thought up her crack-brained scheme to blackmail Sam Thorn, this wouldn't be happening. John wouldn't even be in Nugget City. She would have gone somewhere else to meet him. But now it was happening, and there wasn't a thing she could do to prevent the drama from being played out to its tragic end, an end that might leave John Brown lying in the street.

Kelso walked slowly, staring straight ahead. He was a despicable man, Cathy thought, the kind of man who was repulsive even to look at. If she had met him on the street, she would have hurried past him, but there would be no hurrying now.

Kelso stopped directly in front of Cathy, one step away from Brown. Without warning, Kelso reached out and, grabbing the cigar from Brown's mouth, threw it into the street, then took a firm grip on the brim of Brown's hat and yanked it down over his eyes. He danced back off the board walk into the street, his voice shrill in jeering laughter.

"That'll teach you, mister," he yelled. "Coming to Nugget City, carrying two guns, and acting big as all hell. Them guns ain't gonna do you a bit of good."

He stopped twenty feet from Brown, silent, waiting, his meaty lips pulled tightly against his teeth in a grin of sorts, his legs spread, his body tense, expectant. Brown pushed his hat back off his forehead, resettled it on his head, then said calmly: "This is a bad day to die, sonny. Think about it while you still have time."

"I ain't the one who's gonna die," Kelso shot back. "You are. Now get up out of that chair and into the street. I don't want nobody else getting hurt."

Brown rose but didn't move off the board walk. He said: "I've met up with quite a few kids like you at one time or another. They're buried from Tacosa to Miles City. I'm telling you again. Think this over, because dying is the most permanent thing you'll ever do, and dying for Sam Thorn ain't worth it. It ain't like you'n me had anything to fight about."

For just a moment Kelso seemed shaken, perhaps wondering how Brown would know of his deal with Thorn, then it passed and bravado took hold of him again. He said: "You're talking for yourself, old man. Let's stop the palaver and get it over with."

A number of people had been on the street and the board walk, but they had disappeared. Cathy noticed this in a strange, detached way, as if she were watching a scene from a play in which she did not have a rôle.

Cathy's whole body was tense, her fists clenched so tightly the nails bit into the palms of her hands. She saw Brown step off the walk into the dust of the street,

146

his gaze never wavering from Kelso's face, his right hand splayed above the butt of the gun he wore on that side of his body. When he reached the middle of the street Kelso went for his gun.

Cathy had turned her head toward him, wanting to scream at him not to do what he had come here to do, but no sound came from her parted lips. She saw Kelso's gun being swept from its holster, she heard the roar of Brown's Colt, a gigantic explosion hammering into the silence, and she watched Kelso being slammed back as if a sudden, great gust of wind too hard to stand against had struck him.

Kelso's gun went off, the barrel still slanted downward, the slug kicking up dust half way between him and Brown. He started to sag at every joint, then he was sprawled out in the street, his hat falling from his head, his red hair tousled and unkempt, blood making a wet spot on the front of his shirt.

Suddenly Cathy began to cry, her head bowed. The tension fled from her body, leaving it weak and limp. Brown stood motionless for several seconds, as if wondering if Kelso had enough life left in his body to pick up the gun that had dropped from his slack fingers, but there was none. He holstered his gun and stepped back onto the board walk.

Suddenly men swarmed into the street, Al Fleming from the hotel, Buck Moore from the store, Morgan from the bank, and even old Doc Cotter hobbled out of his office, and others. Cotter took only a second to kneel beside Kelso and feel for a pulse, then he struggled to his feet, Fleming reaching down and giving him a hand.

"Where's the sheriff?" Cotter demanded. "He ought to be on hand when we have a killing."

"Rode out of town half an hour ago or more," Fleming said. "We'd better send the body out to the Rafter E. He was Pete Egan's man."

"Been riding high ever since he hit town," Lobo Wells, the Silver Star bartender, said. "Been asking for this, but nobody would accommodate him."

"None of us had the guts to take him on," Buck Moore said.

For a time no one moved or said anything, then Moore cleared his throat. "Well, we can't leave his carcass in the street. Al, go get a team and wagon from the livery stable. I'll have Joe drive him out to the Rafter E. I can get along without him in the store for a while. We'll let Pete decide what to do with his remains."

"He'll bury him out there," Doc Cotter said. "He's got his own little cemetery back of the house, up on the hill."

Fleming strode toward the livery stable. Buck Moore turned his eyes to Brown, and Brown, apparently sensing what was in his mind, said: "I'll stay in town and talk to the sheriff when he gets back. I figger he'll want to see me."

Moore nodded, obviously relieved because he hadn't had to press the point with Brown. He said: "It's my guess he won't hold you. Kelso's been spoiling for trouble ever since Egan brought him here."

148

"He finally got more'n he could handle," Wells said.

"If the sheriff gives you any trouble," Moore said to Brown, "send him to me. I watched the whole thing. I couldn't make out the talk, but it appeared to me that Kelso forced the fight onto you. I know he drew first."

"Yeah, he forced it, all right," Brown said. "I had no reason to kill him. Never saw him before."

"I don't know who you are, or why you're here," Moore said, "but you've got the fastest draw I ever seen, and we've had some pretty fair gunslingers in Nugget City."

He walked away, crossing the street to the front door of his store. Cathy had stopped crying, but she still sat motionless, as if frozen in her chair, her head down.

"Let's go to your place," Brown said as he stood up. "I'm sorry you had to see this."

She rose, her face white, and reached out to grip his arm. "If it had to happen, I'm not sorry I saw it," she said in a low voice. "At least I didn't have to wait and worry about whether you're alive or dead."

They walked slowly along the board walk, not glancing at the group of men surrounding Kelso's body. She did not look back until they reached her house, and, when she did, she saw a wagon leave the livery stable and turn to where Kelso's body lay.

When they were inside, she led the way back to the kitchen and dropped into a chair beside the table. Brown followed her, asking: "Where's that bottle you had the other day?"

"In the pantry," she said.

He brought it and two glasses to the table and poured a stiff drink into each. "Here," he said, shoving one glass toward her. "You need this."

She seldom drank any kind of liquor, but she was still weak, her hands trembling, so she decided he was right. She picked the glass up and took one swallow, then shuddered as the whiskey hit her stomach. She set the glass down and lifted her head, her gaze on Brown's face.

"I'm sorry, John," she said.

"About what?"

"About getting you into this," she answered. "And for my crazy dream that's not going to do anything for us. You could have been killed today."

Brown shook his head, a slight smile on his lips. "Not by that red-headed kid. I've been down this road so many times it's getting monotonous. It wasn't just that Kelso wanted to cut another notch on his gun. It was our banker friend who wanted me killed so much he hired the kid to try. That means I've got to call on the banker pretty soon."

"No." She reached out to grip his hands. "We've been through enough, John. Let's take the stage to Gunnison in the morning. I've saved a little money. Enough to go somewhere else. New Mexico. Arizona. Anywhere that's away from here. I'll open another shop and you can find a job. You'd be a good lawman."

"Me, wear a star?" He went around the table and sat down beside her. "That's the craziest thing I ever heard."

She took a long breath. "You'll find something. Right now, all I want is to leave here."

"I ain't leaving here yet," Brown said stubbornly. "I never walk off from an unfinished job, and this one sure ain't finished. It won't be until I clean Thorn's plow for him."

"John, I don't want to go on with . . ."

"It ain't your scheme now," he broke in. "That bastard tried to get me killed. I'm going to make him sorry he ever thought about it."

Cathy stared at him, sick with regret, sick with frustration, but knowing there was nothing she could do to make him change his mind. He was a good man in most ways, but she had always been aware of his exaggerated pride and stubbornness.

"You're a difficult man, John Brown," she said. "Are you always going to live by an eye for an eye and a . . ."

"I know the rest of it," he said impatiently. "That is the way I've always lived, and the way I've got to live. I ain't sure I'll get your five thousand dollars for you, but I'm going to scare Thorn to death. Before I'm done with him, he'll wish he'd given you the money."

"I don't know, John," she said worriedly. "I don't know if I can live the rest of my life like this, always worrying about you." She paused, smiling, then added: "But then, I love you so much I can't live without you."

"We have to live our own way," he said. "You know me pretty well, so you won't be surprised after we're married. I can't change, Cathy. Any greedy son of a bitch of a banker who hires a man to kill me is worse

151

than the man who pulls the trigger because he's such a coward he won't try it himself."

"But you're going to do something that will set the sheriff after you," she cried. "There's no reason for that."

"I don't aim to do no such thing," he said. "I like your friend, McCoy, and I've seen mighty few star-toters I ever liked. He ain't old enough to be pig-headed and think he's the judge, the law, and God all rolled into one."

"Well, what are we going to do?" she asked. "I'll follow you anywhere. I can't do anything else."

He rose and walked to a window. He stood there a long moment, staring at the sharp peaks that rose above the foothills. Finally he said: "I know you don't like it here, but I think maybe I would. If you were married, you wouldn't worry about what the women think of you, and you wouldn't be trying to satisfy 'em, making their dresses. With Thorn gone, and I figure he will be by the time I'm done with him, it might be a good place to live."

Surprised, she asked: "Just what is there in this horrible little town that you like?"

"It's out of the way," he said. "Quiet. Or was before I got here. I think I'd like the men if I got to know them. They didn't get down on me because I'd killed Kelso. The storekeeper even said he'd tell the sheriff how it happened." He turned from the window to look at her. "I ain't good with words, Cathy, and maybe I don't say I love you often enough, but I do, and I'll try to make you happy, wherever we go." He stopped and cleared his throat. "The fact is, I'm just tired of running. I've got a lot of men in my past who'd like to kill me, but I don't think they'd find me here. I reckon that's why some of the people who are here came in the first place."

She rose and, going to him, clung to him as if afraid to let go. She had wanted to hear him say he loved her for so long, but he had never said the words before. With her face pressed against his shirt, she said: "I don't care whether we stay here or go somewhere else. I just want to be with you."

He put his arms around her and held her. She knew he was a man who would never live in peace, no matter where he was, but she knew that it would be her way of life, too. She had no choice.

CHAPTER
NINETEEN

Ed McCoy returned to Nugget City late in the afternoon. When he reached the hotel, he saw that John Brown was not sitting in the chair he had occupied for so many hours. He had been in that chair long enough to give Ed the feeling that something was missing, now that he wasn't there. He reined in toward the hotel, dismounted, and tied up his horse.

The lobby was empty, but Al Fleming heard him and came in through the dining room door.

"Where's Brown?" Ed asked.

"Dunno." Fleming shifted his weight uneasily. "He left a while ago with Cathy Allen." He cleared his throat, then added: "I guess you wouldn't have heard, being gone from town all afternoon, but he shot and killed Red Mike Kelso a little while ago."

"The hell." Ed backed up to a chair set against the street wall of the lobby and sat down. "What happened? Did Brown provoke a fight?"

"Wasn't his fault, as near as I could figure out," Fleming said. "I didn't know Kelso was in town till I heard him yelling at Brown. Something about them guns not doing Brown any good." He jerked his head toward the dining room. "I'd been in there, fixing the tables for supper, when I heard the yell, so I came out here to see what was going on." He shook his head. "I don't know what got into Kelso. He's been proddy ever since he hit town, but today he was downright nasty. I didn't see the first of it, but afterwards, Buck told me . . . he'd been watching the whole thing from across the street . . . he said Kelso came up, jerked Brown's cigar out of his mouth, and pulled his hat down over his eyes. Just like a bratty kid trying to get somebody's attention. Well, he got it, all right.

"Brown stood up, tried to talk some sense into Kelso, but there wasn't no use. Kelso was just spoiling for his fight. He drew first, but, hell, he didn't have no chance. I never seen a faster draw than Brown showed us today. Kelso never got a decent shot off. His gun was still pointing at the ground when he pulled the trigger. I guess he was dead while he was still on his feet." He shook his head. "By God, Ed, don't you ever go up against Brown or we'll be needing a new sheriff."

"So he's as good as you'd expect a two-gun man would be," Ed said. "Wonder why we never heard of him before?"

"There's a lot of men good with their guns that we don't hear about," Fleming said. "The famous ones ain't necessarily the best. Depends on who the newspapers write up, where a man is, and who he's killed."

Fleming stared thoughtfully through the open door into the street, then he added: "It does make me feel better in one way. Brown's a man you'd have to shoot in the back to get an edge on him. On the other hand,

155

a man like him ain't likely to come here to murder me. I don't think he's that kind of *hombre*."

"Nothing was said about why Kelso was so hell-bent on getting into a fight?"

Fleming shook his head. "Not a word. He plain just rode into town, wanting to kick up some dust. I don't know how you see it, but I don't think you've got anything to hold Brown on. Sure was a plain case of self-defense."

Ed rose. "I guess I ain't surprised. Kelso hits town, makes some brags about how good he is, but then, when Brown shows up, he don't say a word, and he turns out better'n Kelso."

"There sure wasn't any question about who was good, and who wasn't," Fleming said.

Ed walked to the door, paused, then asked: "What happened to the body?"

"Buck Moore kind of took charge," Fleming answered, "seeing you weren't here. Told me to go fetch a wagon from the stable, and we loaded the body into it, then Buck had Joe Walker drive it out to the Rafter E. Kelso's horse was tied in front of the Silver Star. I don't know why Buck just didn't have the body tied down across the saddle. Joe could've led his horse out to the Rafter E."

"Well, we'll be hearing from Pete Egan before long," Ed said. "Now he will be convinced that Curt Maulden sent for Brown, and he'll raise hell."

"Yep." Fleming nodded. "I wish Brown had never thought about coming to Nugget City."

156

Ed McCoy crossed the street, not doubting Fleming's version of what had happened, but thinking that he needed two stories before he saw Brown. The question rose again in his mind that Fleming's remark had aroused. Why had Brown come here? He'd know sooner or later, but it gnawed at him because he needed the answer now, if he was going to head off more serious trouble. He had a hunch he wasn't going to have it in time.

Moore was standing in the doorway of his store when Ed reached him. Moore said: "I thought you'd be over as soon as you finished talking to Al. I reckon he told you what happened?"

Ed nodded. "I just want to see how your version jibes with Al's."

"I know more about it than Al does," the storekeeper said. "I just happened to be sweeping off the walk when Kelso rode in. I never seen a man spoiling for a fight the way Kelso was."

When he finished telling what he had seen, Ed nodded. "Looks like Brown's in the clear. Wasn't much else he could do."

Moore nodded. "Not unless he turned around and walked into the hotel, and you couldn't expect a man of his caliber to do that. Anyhow, the way Kelso was performing, he'd probably have gone right in after him."

"Probably would have," Ed agreed. "Funny thing. You seem to be taking Brown's side."

"I'm not on anybody's side," Moore snapped. "I'm just telling you what happened, but, if I had to be on somebody's side, it would be Brown's. He hasn't bothered nobody since he got here, but that damned Kelso was on the prod from the day he rode into town. I've been sore at Egan ever since for bringing him in. Pete didn't need him, and the community didn't need him." He pointed a finger at Ed, jabbing the air with it. "I'll tell you something else, Ed. I'm damned tired of Maulden's and Egan's feuding and upsetting the whole county when it's a private fight which probably didn't have a real cause in the first place."

"I know," Ed nodded. "They'd probably deny it's got anything to do with upsetting the county, but I know it does. I'm expecting Pete to show up in town and kick up some trouble when he hears Kelso got himself killed."

"That's just what I've been thinking," Moore said. "Somebody might get hurt. What are you going to do about it?"

"I'm one man," Ed said angrily, "and the county does not see fit to hire a deputy. Pete'll bring half a dozen or more men with him. If Curly Wilson decides that the M Bar needs to make a move, he'll bring three or four. If they hit here at the same time, the town will get shot to pieces. How much help will I get from you or Al or Doc Cotter or anybody else?"

"Chances are, none," Moore said. "Old Fist never asked for no help."

"He had a bunch of deputies," Ed reminded him.

"It was different in those days," Moore said harshly. "You don't have a tough mining town to ride herd on.

You knew the situation when you took the star. You're paid to handle situations like this."

Ed stared at Moore for several seconds, fury tugging at his tongue. He had never heard Moore talk this way before. The storekeeper was usually a soft-spoken, courteous man, but this was a different Buck Moore. Suddenly he saw something in the man's face he had never seen before, a stark, soul-shaking fear. He had seen a man die a few minutes before, but it was more than that, Ed thought, more than the fear of his own safety.

"You're scared, Buck," Ed said. "Why?"

"I'm scared about what's going to happen," Moore said somberly. "I don't think you can keep the lid on. I don't want Nugget City to be a battleground, and I figger that's what's going to happen. This damn' feud is about to break out into a real fight." Moore stared into the street for a moment, then brought his gaze back to Ed's face. "I started getting scared the day Kelso showed. He bragged all over town about Pete hiring him. Well, he's gone, but Pete'll fetch his crew with him when he figgers it's time. Or maybe hire a bunch of gunfighters. Men like this Brown. I know Curt ain't much of a threat now, but Curly Wilson is."

"I'll handle it," Ed said and, turning on his heel, left the store.

He felt both anger and pity for the storekeeper, anger because Moore had made it plain that he didn't think Ed could fill his dad's shoes in a crisis, and pity because the man was afraid to accept his duty as a citizen. As he untied his roan and swung into the saddle, he recalled that there had been times when his father had needed a posse, and he'd never had trouble finding men to make up that posse, but the town men had been a different breed then, not the Moores and Flemings and crippled-up old men like Doc Cotter.

He rode down the street to Cathy Allen's house, telling himself that Nugget City was different now, conditions were different, times were different, but he also realized that he wasn't Fist McCoy, and that made a hell of a lot of difference. There might come a day when people would feel the confidence in him they'd had in his father, but that day wasn't now. It wouldn't be here until he had proved he could fill Fist McCoy's shoes. The way events were moving, that day might be tomorrow.

Dismounting, he left his horse ground hitched and walked up the path to the house. Cathy opened the door to his knock, smiled, and said: "Come in, Sheriff. We've been expecting you."

He stepped inside, as he took off his hat, and followed her through her work room into the kitchen where Brown was sitting at the table, drinking coffee. He nodded to Ed, his face as bleak and dour as ever.

"I guess you've heard," Brown said.

"I've heard," Ed said.

Cathy motioned to a chair at the table. "Sit down. I'll pour you a cup of coffee."

Ed took the chair, wondering if Brown was worried and decided he wasn't, although the gunman would not let it show in his face if he were. Ed watched Cathy bring a cup from the pantry to the stove, fill it with coffee, and place the cup in front of him.

"I'd like to hear your version of what happened," Ed said.

Brown gave it to him, with Cathy nodding her head in agreement. Ed glanced at her when Brown finished. "That the way you saw it?" he asked.

"Yes," she said, "except that John didn't tell you how Kelso acted. He was like a spoiled child who doesn't get what he wants, or the attention he thinks he deserves. I never saw a grown man perform that way. It was just . . . just . . . ridiculous."

Brown shrugged. "He wanted a fight and that was the only way he could think of. It was like those old duels we used to read about when one man slaps the other man across the face with his glove. I didn't have any reason to quarrel with Kelso, so he had to do something to give me a reason." He chewed on his lower lip a moment, eyes boring into Ed. "What would you have done, Sheriff?"

"Probably what you did," Ed answered. "I'm not holding you, in case you're wondering how I feel about it. I talked to Al Fleming and Buck Moore. Their stories agree with yours. A funny thing is happening, Brown. You scared folks just by showing up, but now I've got a feeling you're a sort of hero to 'em. Kelso wasn't liked by anybody, even Pete Egan. Kelso tried to be a big man, and I suppose he could have gunned down anybody who lived around here, but he didn't make any friends by being braggy and insolent." He sipped his coffee, watching Brown over the brim of his cup. He added: "Another funny thing, if Buck Moore is typical of others in town, and I'm guessing he is, folks are afraid of what will happen between the Rafter E and the M Bar."

"Fear is like measles, Sheriff," Brown said. "It's catching."

"That's right," Ed agreed, "and there is some reason for 'em to be afraid, though I ain't sure it'll happen here in town. That's what's making Moore stew. I'm guessing that killing Kelso is going to make Egan mad enough to go after Maulden, figuring you're Maulden's man. He'll include anybody else he thinks is on Maulden's side. That's where the town will get into trouble. Curt's crazy, but he's got more friends in the county than Egan has."

Brown spread his hands as if he didn't understand what was happening. "Looks to me like this is a town with scared people. I savvy why Cathy hates it here."

"If I'd known when I first came here what I know now," Cathy said, "I never would have stayed."

"Brown, how'd you like to serve as my deputy till this is over?" Ed asked.

"Me?" Brown said. "I never pinned on a star in my life. I'll think about it. Cathy says I'd . . ."

A loud rap brought Cathy to her feet. "I'll see who it is," she said, and left the room.

"It'll be Pete Egan," Ed said.

A moment later she was back. "I looked through the window. It is Pete Egan."

"Bring him in," Ed said, and nodded at Brown. "Don't make me any more trouble than I've got."

CHAPTER
TWENTY

Sam Thorn waited at his office window, hoping to see Red Mike Kelso ride by. He grew more impatient by the minute as the afternoon slipped by, and he began to wonder if he had wasted the money he had paid Kelso. Maybe the gunman didn't have the guts to face Brown; maybe he was just wind.

Thorn had an angled-window view of Main Street, the Silver Star Saloon the only building on the other side of the street that he could see clearly. It was possible that Kelso had ridden past without Thorn's seeing him, so occasionally he stepped into the bank lobby, finding one excuse after another. He didn't want Morgan to guess that he had any interest in Kelso. He always took time to glance at the front of the hotel. John Brown was there all afternoon.

Just when he was giving up on Kelso, the gunman arrived, dismounting and tying at the hitch pole in front of the Silver Star. Thorn heaved a sigh of relief, the tension that had become intolerable easing and relaxing his body. He thought at first he would stay in his office, not leaving it until he heard the gun shots, but he couldn't stand the suspense. *To hell with what Morgan thought!*

Thorn ran to the door, yanked it open, and hurried to the street window. By then Kelso had almost reached Brown. Thorn saw the gunman stop in front of Cathy Allen and lean forward to yank the cigar out of Brown's mouth and throw it into the street, then pull his hat down over his eyes.

Thorn swore. If he had been in Kelso's boots, he'd have thought of a better way than that of provoking a fight. Kelso was more kid than man, and what he had just done was a kid's way. Thorn watched him back into the street and yell something, but he could not make out the words.

Morgan joined Thorn, curious about what was going on. When he saw that Kelso was trying to provoke a fight, he said: "Is Kelso crazy? He's committing suicide."

Thorn didn't answer, hardly hearing what Morgan said. What happened then was such a nightmare he almost could not believe what he saw. Apparently Brown was trying to talk Kelso out of a fight, but, when he didn't succeed, he stepped into the street, and Kelso started to draw. Brown's gun was in his hand and firing. Thorn would have sworn the gun jumped out of the holster to meet his downsweeping hand. Thorn had seen gun fights before, but he had never seen a draw like Brown's.

Thorn's gaze whipped to Kelso. He was falling as a man falls when he has lost all control, every joint giving way until he sprawled into the dust. *He was dead.* Thorn did not have the slightest doubt. He had pulled the trigger of his gun, but the bullet had driven harmlessly into the street dirt in front of him. The shot had not been aimed. Rather, it had been fired by the jerking spasm of a dying man.

John Brown was alive. Thorn didn't care one way or the other about Kelso, but *Brown was still alive.* The knowledge shocked Thorn, and scared him, and sent a chill through his body that made it start to tremble as if he had the ague.

"I'll be damned," Morgan said wide eyed. "Kelso *did* commit suicide. What the hell was he thinking about?" Thorn turned toward his office door, his face ashen, his step uncertain. Morgan grabbed his arm. "What's the matter, Mister Thorn?"

The banker jerked free and tottered across the lobby, staggering, swaying, as oblivious as if he were walking in his sleep.

Morgan followed, not knowing what to say or do. He repeated: "What's the matter, Mister Thorn?"

Thorn entered his office, shutting the door in Morgan's face. He sat down at his desk, scarcely able to grasp the truth. *John Brown was still alive.* The knowledge kept hammering at his mind as continually as a pulse beat. Cathy Allen had told him Brown would be coming to see him. Now the man would certainly come, just as the woman had said.

Frustration, anger, fear — they all piled up in Sam Thorn until he completely unraveled. He put his head on his arms on the desk and cried as he had not cried since he was a child, cried in moaning sobs until Morgan opened the door and asked in a frightened voice: "Can I do anything, Mister Thorn?"

"Goddamn it, just let me alone," Thorn managed in a muffled voice.

Morgan drew back and shut the door. The moment passed, and slowly composure and sanity returned to Thorn. What could he do? He would not give Brown the money the Allen woman had demanded. That was his worst thought. The one plan he had depended on to keep Brown off his back had failed. Now he had to have another.

He opened a desk drawer and lifted a short-barrel .38 Colt from it and laid it on the desk. He would shoot Brown the minute he stepped through the door. He would tell young McCoy that Brown had tried to rob him. McCoy would certainly believe him instead of a stranger, if he lived long enough to talk.

He drew a bandanna from a back pocket, wiped his eyes, then blew his nose. His mind was working now as sharply and coherently as ever. He knew he was a smart man, a cunning man although that did not quite fit his self image.

The important part was that he had always believed in himself. He was confident that, given time, he could work himself out of any difficult situation. The trouble was he didn't have much time. He would kill Brown, but now, thinking about it rationally, he realized that trying to shoot Brown when the gunman came into his office would not work. He would be committing suicide as surely as Red Mike Kelso had.

No, there had to be a better plan. He picked up the revolver, saw that five shells were in the cylinder, and laid it back in the drawer. He had only fired the gun a

166

few times. The truth was he had never felt comfortable with firearms, but he had bought the Colt in case he faced an attempted robbery. He had always intended to go out of town somewhere and practice shooting, but he had kept putting it off, and now, when he needed gun skill, he didn't have it.

Still, if he could catch Brown at close range when the gunman wasn't expecting trouble, he could shoot well enough to kill him. He had no qualms about shooting the man in the back. What the Allen woman and Brown were planning was extortion, and extortion was another word for robbery. Killing Brown would not bother his conscience, and even McCoy would have to admit it was justifiable homicide.

Confidence began flowing back into Thorn. He considered his options. Probably Brown spent his time in the Allen woman's house. He would likely eat his next meal there. If Thorn survived the afternoon meeting with Brown, he would go home as usual, eat supper, and, when it was dark, go to the Allen woman's house. Sooner or later Brown would leave and he'd have a chance to shoot him and escape in the darkness.

He thought about leaving now and telling Morgan to lock up at six, but, if he went home, he would have to think up something to tell Myra. He would be forced to be with her until he could say he had to work at the bank, and then she would ask why hadn't he stayed that afternoon to finish it?

More than thinking up explanations, the thought of just being with Myra for several hours was too much to bear. Besides, he didn't want to make excuses to

167

Morgan, so he'd wait here until six and close the bank himself as he usually did.

He felt better now that he had a plan. He had plenty of work to do. For more than a year he had carefully scheduled a timetable for closing out the various ranches and farms that were mortgaged. Most of these people were behind in their interest payments. It was a question of which place best fitted into the pattern he had laid out. He was not a farmer, and he had to be careful not to take a place away from its owner until he had a man in mind to run it for him.

A tap on the door broke into his thinking. Irritably he called: "What is it?" *Damn Morgan!* he told himself. *The man had to run to him for every decision when he could make most of them himself.*

"Miss York is here to see you," Morgan called.

What in the hell was Sally doing here? he asked himself. He didn't want to see her now, but he couldn't risk sending her away. Sally York was the one person in Marion County he didn't want to offend.

He rose, crossed the room to the door, and opened it. Sally York stood smiling at him. She was not an attractive woman in the way Cathy Allen was attractive but still good looking to him because he loved her, and she loved him, and to Sam Thorn that had been something of a miracle.

"Why, Sally, it's nice of you to stop by," he said as he stepped back and motioned for her to come in.

She was wearing a tight-fitting dress, one that was not appropriate, he thought and told himself he would have to speak to her about it. The dress would have

168

been just right for a whore in a mining camp, but for a school teacher in Nugget City it was scandalous.

She walked past him into the office, saying nothing, and took a chair across the desk from him. She still didn't say a word as he moved back to his desk and sat down, her knees drawn up demurely, her feet flat on the floor, her reticule held by both hands on her lap.

Thorn sat down, opened his cigar box, and took one from it. He bit off the end, his gaze on her face. *Something was wrong,* he thought. He had always discouraged her coming to the bank to see him, and she had never done it before. Now, looking at her thin face, he sensed something different, something unpleasant. It was in her eyes, in the way her lips were squeezed together so tightly they formed a narrow red line. Suddenly he noticed they were much brighter red than usual, and he realized she had painted them. He had never known her to do that before. He'd have to speak to her about that, too.

"Well, my dear," he said as he fished for a match in his vest pocket, "to what do I owe this unexpected pleasure?"

"I'm leaving on the stage tomorrow morning," she said in a matter-of-fact tone. "I have mailed a letter of resignation to you so you will have ample time to find another teacher before school opens. In view of the services I have rendered to you in the past year, I want one thousand dollars. It is a very meager payment, considering the type of service I have given you in my bed, but I don't like greedy people, so I'll settle for enough to set me up in business somewhere else."

169

Thorn dropped his hand from his vest pocket. The other hand that gripped the cigar went slack, the cigar turning slightly as it fell from his hand. He stared at her, totally rejecting what she had just said and certainly not believing it. Of all the days, for her to come here and say anything as preposterous as this, today it was too much. She must have something in mind, something she wanted him to do. Perhaps divorce Myra and marry her.

"I have been under a great deal of pressure today," he said slowly, "and I am in no mood to hear jokes. Now, tell me exactly what you have in mind."

"Just what I told you," she said. "Nothing more and nothing less. I've resigned. I'm packed, and I am waiting impatiently to leave in the morning. How I have been able to live this long in a town as ugly and horrible as Nugget City is more than I know. Now I can't wait to leave."

"You actually mean what you're saying?" he asked incredulously. "I don't believe you really mean it."

"Oh, I mean it, all right," she said. "What have I got to say to make you believe it?"

"We've meant too much to each other," he said in that same incredulous tone. "You're the only woman I ever loved. You love me. I just can't believe you could cut it off like this."

"Love you?" She laughed softly. "Sam, I've never loved you. I'm not a good teacher, but I'm a hell of a good whore. I've never even enjoyed going to bed with you, but part of being a good whore is being a good

170

actress. I've fooled a lot of men, just like I fooled you. Now give me my money."

"You've been a whore?" he whispered. "I don't believe it."

She shrugged. "Believe it or not. I wouldn't ever have come here if I hadn't got into trouble with the police in Denver. This was a good place to hide, and, when I found out that you needed a teacher, I applied. I looked the part, and I've acted the part, but I've hated every minute when I was pretending to love all those snot-nosed little brats. I've stayed long enough for the police to lose interest in me, but I can't risk going back to Denver, so I'll go to Cripple Creek. It's a good camp. It won't shut down like the silver camps have."

He was numb. How could his world have dissolved the way it had today? Only a few hours ago everything had been right, but now too many things had happened — his fright when he had been afraid the gunman knew of his past, the Allen woman's extortion scheme, Kelso's death, the knowledge that the gunman would be coming here, maybe to kill him, and now this from the one woman he had learned to trust and love. Yes, love.

"I can't see why you're doing this now," he said dully.

"I had intended to stay longer," she admitted, "but, when this Brown showed up, I knew it was time to go. He hasn't recognized me, but he will if I stay. I guess I'd rather leave here with people thinking of me as a teacher rather than as a whore."

"You . . . say . . . you . . . never . . . loved . . . me?" he asked in a forlorn voice, wanting to hear her say she did, hoping she had said those things without really meaning them.

"Hell, no," she snapped. "Now, by God, I'll tell you one more time. I gave you the best service a whore ever gave a man, and I want to be paid."

This *was* a nightmare. He rose. It couldn't be happening. He remained certain that he would wake up and find out it was only a bad dream. He was walking toward her. He knew he was sleepwalking, that some other mind, some other power was propelling him toward her, telling him what to do. She watched him, suddenly alarmed, and, when he was three feet away, she tried to get out of her chair, but she had waited too long.

His big hands gripped her by the throat and began to squeeze.

CHAPTER
TWENTY-ONE

Ed and John Brown stood beside the table when Cathy led Pete into the kitchen. He stopped just inside the door, an angry, red-faced man, his gaze pinned on Brown's face. He was wearing his gun, but he carefully kept his right hand away from its butt.

"So you're the *hombre* who killed Mike Kelso," Egan said, his tone a statement of fact rather than a question.

Brown nodded. "That's right. Have you asked anyone what brought on our fight?"

"No, and I ain't figuring on doing it," Egan said. "It don't make no difference what caused the fight. What does make a difference is that for years I've thought I'd have a showdown with Curt Maulden. That's why I hired Kelso. Now I don't have him."

"I talked to Curt this afternoon," Ed said. "You won't be fighting him. I hadn't seen him for a while, but he's worse off than I thought he was."

Egan waved the words away with a motion of his right hand. "Don't make no difference and you know it. If it ain't Curt, it'd be Curly Wilson. What I'm saying is that this gent killed the man I counted on as insurance when I have a showdown with the M Bar."

173

"There won't be a showdown unless you make one," Ed said.

"There's a gonna be a showdown the minute my water stops flowing," Egan shot back, "and you know it."

"I told Curt I'd arrest him the minute he diverted your water," Ed said.

Egan snorted. "You're a bigger fool than I thought you were, McCoy. If Maulden is as loco as you say he is, he didn't even hear you." He turned his gaze back to Brown. "How'd you like to work for me, one hundred dollars a month, same as I was paying Red Mike?"

Brown shook his head. "Your boys would run me off the place."

"If you want the job," Egan said, "I'll see there won't be no trouble between you and the others."

Brown shook his head again. "Me'n Cathy are leaving town in a day or two."

Egan jerked his head at Ed. "See? Don't tell me that Maulden or Wilson didn't bring this man here. They knew Red Mike would jump this gunman, and they wanted Mike dead before they'd feel safe turning the water off."

"Oh, hell," Brown said in disgust. "I'm hearing an echo. That other *hombre*, Wilson, I guess it was, said the same thing, only he turned it around."

"That's right, Pete," Ed said. "You both insist on thinking Brown's working for the other man. Well, neither one of you sent for him. I wish you'd get that through your head."

Egan scowled, his gaze whipping from one man to the other, then he said slowly: "I've tried not to bring on a range war, figuring I would outlast Maulden, but I can't risk losing my water even for a day at this time of year, so I'm taking my boys through your goddamned town, and we're riding up the valley, and we'll blow Maulden's dam to hell and gone. He's had it built for years, just ready to fill in and ruin me. Well, I ain't waiting for him to do it." Egan jabbed the air with a forefinger aimed at Ed. "Don't try to stop me or we'll ride you down."

He wheeled and strode out of the house, not waiting to hear Ed call: "Don't try it, Pete. I told you I'd take care of it."

The front door slammed.

Brown said: "Well, Sheriff, when a man builds up enough hate and meanness, he starts using guns, and then there ain't a bit of reason left in him. I guess that's what starts wars." He eyed Ed a moment, then went on. "Cathy says I'd make a good lawman, but I've never been on that side of the fence. Not because I ever robbed a bank or anything like that, but because the wrong people always seemed to control the law. That don't seem to be happening here."

"It ain't," Ed said. "I just inherited a feud, and your coming to town fanned the coals into a fire. Both of 'em insist on thinking your showing up here means the other one's fixing to start the ball."

"How many men will Egan bring with him?" Brown asked.

"I dunno," Ed admitted. "Six, eight. He could bring more, but I doubt that he'll fetch his whole crew. I'm guessing he won't think he needs that many. Besides, they're too busy right now to pull all of 'em off their jobs."

"It'll be more'n one man can handle," Brown said.

Ed nodded. "It may mean my funeral, but he'll lead 'em right through town to show everybody I ain't a big enough man to do my job, then he'll go on up the creek to the M Bar and raise hell."

"How much will the deputy job pay?" Brown asked.

"Thirty a month," Ed answered, "if I can get the money."

Brown grinned. "And I just turned down a job for a hundred dollars a month. Well, I guess I'm to blame for what's happening around here, so I'd better give you a hand in the morning."

"I could use it," Ed said and, nodding to Cathy, left the house.

He mounted his roan and rode home, the late-afternoon sun throwing a long shadow of horse and rider onto the dust beside him. He wondered about the relationship between Cathy Allen and John Brown. The man was old enough to be her father, but there was certainly no daughter-father feeling between them.

He watered and fed his horse, turning the problem over in his mind. The showdown between Egan and Maulden would have come sooner or later, but Brown's coming to Nugget City had brought it to a head and all because of Maulden's and Egan's suspicion of each other.

There was little he could do by himself to turn Egan's outfit back, but he had to try. With Brown's help, he might succeed. One thing was in his favor. Egan was sane. He could be reasoned with, or at least he could be made to understand the risks he would take if he tried to ride Ed down, especially with Brown standing beside him.

Supper was ready when he went into the house. Judy saw him coming and ran to meet him before he reached the kitchen, hugging and kissing him with a passion he had never felt in her before.

"Let him eat his supper, Judy," Mrs McCoy called from where she was setting a bowl of gravy on the table. "I never seen no much hugging and kissing in all my born days as I have since I found you on the back porch."

Judy turned away from Ed and walked back into the kitchen. "I didn't know if he was alive or not," she said in an irritated tone she seldom used. "I know my father better than you do."

Mrs McCoy stared at her, surprised by Judy's sharp reaction. Ed hid a grin as he turned to the wash stand and pumped water into the basin, thinking that Judy would have to show this kind of spunk more often or his mother would run over her as long as she lived.

"Yes, I guess you do," Mrs McCoy said.

Judy went to the table, silent until Ed sat down. Mrs McCoy brought a platter of steak to the table and took her chair at the head, then Judy, unable to hold back any longer, demanded: "Ed, I want to know what happened."

"The first thing I want to tell you is that your father is more concerned about you than you've been thinking," Ed said as he helped himself to the meat. "The second thing is that he's afraid of Curly. The third thing is that he performed about the way you've been saying he would. He was rational and downright friendly most of the time I was there, though he had me confused with my dad at first. It was only when I mentioned the dam and Pete Egan that he turned into a maniac. After that, I was lucky to get out of there alive."

She nodded. "He's dwelt on his hatred of Egan so long that it's made him crazy. I didn't know anyone could be that way, sane and insane at the same time. I mean, not really at the same time, but rather a few seconds apart. Anything that applies to a normal man simply does not apply to him when he's incensed about Egan."

Ed told her the details of what had happened when he was at the M Bar, finishing with: "I guess what surprised me the most was how concerned he was about you when he was talking sense. We had a good visit, and he didn't blame you for leaving. He remembered when you stayed here and that ma taught you how to cook. He even told me to take good care of you, or he'd go after me with a blacksnake."

He was silent for a time as he ate, not sure how much Judy was able to accept about Curly, then decided he had to tell her what Curt had said. "Your pa told me that Curly has always been loco about you and had been the same about your ma. He said Curly had been waiting a long time for you to grow up, and that Curly wasn't the man everybody thought he was." Ed paused, still not sure how Judy would take this. He went on slowly: "Judy, it strikes me that Curly is in love with you. He wants to marry you, and he won't stop at anything till he gets what he wants. Your pa is whacky some of the time, but I believe he's right about Curly."

Judy put down her fork and stared at Ed in disbelief. "You are as . . ." She stopped herself before she finished saying what she had started to say. She looked down at her plate, bit her lower lip as if holding back words she wanted to say, then raised her head and said defiantly: "You're wrong, Ed. Curly has been a good friend. Nothing more."

Ed knew that she couldn't see Curly Wilson the way he saw him, and she probably wouldn't for a long time. He shrugged his shoulders to dismiss the subject, then said: "Well, Curt was able to talk rationally for a long time, and he was able to tell me how worried he was about you. He said that now you were my responsibility, and it was up to me to take care of you." He paused, knowing that now he had to say something else with which she wouldn't agree. "I aim to take care of you. Tomorrow I'd better take you to the Abbots' place. You'll be safe there. Old Monk would give his life for you if it came to that."

Her gaze had been on his face all the time he was talking. Now she said as defiantly as before: "I won't go. I'm perfectly safe right here. Curly would never harm me."

Ed shoved his plate back, part of his supper still on it. He didn't feel like finishing it. How could he take care of a woman who wouldn't be taken care of? His duties as sheriff seemed minor when compared to this personal one.

"We'll try to keep you safe," Mrs McCoy said, "but sometimes things happen we can't foresee. Ed just wants to make sure that nothing like that happens to you. I'm sure that Curly has been a good friend to you, but he may . . ."

Judy rose. "I'm tired. I guess I didn't get much sleep last night."

She left the kitchen and went upstairs to her room, her face pale. Ed's gaze followed her until she was out of sight, then he sighed. "Damn a stubborn woman. I can't hit her, I can't tie her up, and I sure as hell can't reason with her."

"That's often a problem in a marriage," his mother said. "Your father used to say the same thing about me." She paused, then added thoughtfully: "I think it's hard for either of us to see Curly through Judy's eyes, but then I think about how her life was after her mother died. Curt was never a demonstrative man, even though he probably loved Judy in his own way. Curly was the one person Judy could turn to, the one person who she knew loved her. She's still got that picture in her mind."

Ed nodded. "I know. Curly may once have thought of Judy as a little sister, but he sure as hell ain't thinking of her that way now. When Judy finds out, if she ever does, it'll tear her apart." He shook his head, frowning. "I dunno, Ma. Sometimes I wonder who is crazy."

"Oh, Curly ain't crazy," Mrs McCoy said quickly. "He's a schemer, but that makes a man mean ornery and just plain dangerous. Not crazy."

Ed rose. "I've got myself a big job tomorrow, and I can't stay home and run herd on Judy. You'll have to do the best you can."

"I've got a shotgun and a rifle," she said. "I'll use them if I have to."

"Keep the house locked up," Ed said. "I don't know what to expect, but Curly might try to get her out of town some way. Maybe he thinks, if he could get her back on the M Bar, she'd be willing to stay. Well, I've got to look the town over."

He picked up his hat from where he had dropped it on the wash stand and left the house.

CHAPTER
TWENTY-TWO

Sam Thorn was shocked back into reality when Sally's body suddenly went limp. Horror stricken, he stepped back and stared at her, unable to believe what he had done. Her head lolled to one side, and then she fell sideways out of her chair and onto the floor. She was dead! He knew it as well as he had ever known anything in his life.

"Sally," he breathed. "I didn't aim to do that to you. I would have given you the money, but why couldn't you have gone on the way we were, even if you were only pretending to love me?"

She didn't answer, and he had not expected an answer. He knelt and felt of her wrist. There wasn't any pulse, but he hadn't expected that, either. Suddenly he realized what would happen if Morgan or someone else came into his office.

Quickly he rose and, striding to the door, turned the key in the lock. He seldom locked the door, and he knew Morgan would wonder about it when he heard the click, but he could not take a chance on Sally's body being discovered.

He returned to his desk and stood, looking down at the dead woman. She was gone. There was nothing he could do to bring her back to life; there was no sense in wishing he hadn't done it, because it was done. All he could do now was to keep people from knowing he had killed her.

Fortunately Sally had no close friends in Nugget City. If he could get her back into her house without being seen, maybe people would think she'd had an accident. At least no one could possibly know that he had killed her.

Turning away, he walked to the window and stood staring at the vacant lot next to the bank. No thought of his loss was in his mind now. After all, Sally had brought this on herself when it had not been necessary. She was not only leaving town and cutting off her relationship with him, but she had tried to extort money from him as well. First the Allen woman and then Sally.

Thorn was never a man to blame himself for anything that went wrong, and he didn't start now. He had given Sally things. He had even laid out money for groceries and rent for her house, but it hadn't been enough. Damn these greedy women. Always wanting more. Actually, it was worse with Sally than with Cathy Allen. Cathy didn't owe him anything. Sally did, but then she was nothing but a common whore, a fact he could not bear even to think about. He had never dreamed she was what she was — and what she wanted to be again.

Sally had lied to him. She had deceived him in the worst way a woman could deceive a man, pretending she loved him, building him up, telling him he was a

183

great man. Well, by God, she deserved what he had given her, but there was little comfort in that. He would miss her, but then he had killed her, and he would hang for it if he was found out.

He couldn't keep his office door locked the rest of the day. Morgan would want to see him before he went home. And that damned gunslinger! Another complication he had forgotten. There was a back door to his office that opened into the alley, and there was a closet in his office.

It would work out, he told himself. He would hide her body in the closet and move it into her home after it was dark. The closet had to do for now. No one ever looked into it. He'd have to take a chance that no one would today.

Picking up Sally's body, he carried it to the closet, surprised at how light she was. Damn it, if she had been a bigger woman . . . like Myra . . . he would not have killed her. He could have squeezed Myra by the throat for an hour, and still she wouldn't die.

He opened the closet door, set the body down inside, Sally's back to one wall, her legs in front of her. Quickly he stepped away from her and closed the door, not wanting to look at her. He would see her in his mind the rest of his life, but at least he did not have to stand there and look at her now.

Thorn returned to his desk and sat down. He had plenty of work to do, but he knew he couldn't focus his mind on it today. He couldn't add the simplest string of figures. How could this have been happening, one thing

184

after another, and all of it since that goddamned gunman had got off the stage?

He'd had his world in order just a few days before. Since he had come to Nugget City, he had slowly gained people's confidence as a good businessman, although some people hated him for his "good business" practices of foreclosing on their homes. On the other hand, he had worked in the church and on the school board, so probably most folks had mixed feelings about him, but the fact remained that nearly everyone in Marion County deposited their money in his bank and came to him for loans, even those as prosperous and powerful as Pete Egan and Curt Maulden.

Over the years he had built a framework for the empire he would control. He had figured it would take another five years before he would be in position to close out Egan and Maulden. They would raise hell and threaten him by bringing their cowhands into town and act as if force would change his decisions, but he knew, and they would know ultimately, it wouldn't work.

The one fly in the ointment of his life was having to live with Myra. He needed to bed down with a woman, but it was impossible any more with Myra, so he'd had to control his passions until he could get to Denver on business, and that had only been two or three times a year. Otherwise his life had been one of complete satisfaction since he had come to Nugget City. Sally had moved here, and it had not taken long to reach an agreement with her which had made him a very contented man.

At first their relationship had been impersonal. She would go to bed with him and he, in turn, as chairman of the school board could promise her a teaching job as long as she wanted it. Later she had, he thought, learned to like him and then love him. She said she did, and, judging her by her actions, he had believed her.

Well, she had fooled him, all right, fooled him so well that for weeks he had been consumed by a lust for her he had never felt for another woman. He had not called it lust. He had thought of it as love. Whichever it had been, he had never been happier in his life. The days always passed too slowly: he could hardly wait until it was dark and time to go to Sally's house.

He had been like a boy with a bad case of puppy love, although he had not recognized it for what it was. It had filled him with a buoyancy, a state of euphoria he had never experienced before. At times he had told himself it had been too good to last. Well, it had been. Now his life had tumbled down around him.

When he'd been a child, he had spent hours placing domino after domino in a row and then tipping the first one over. They had all gone down in a matter of seconds. That was exactly what had happened to all the satisfactions of life that he had earned. Now they were gone, and he faced a hangman's rope.

By God, he still did have a chance, he told himself fiercely. He wasn't down yet. He retained the trust of his customers, the church people, the school board members. People still feared him and his power, and, as long as they feared him, they would believe him. If he could just get Sally's body out of here without anyone

186

seeing it, he'd be in the clear. And, of course, get that infernal gunman and Cathy Allen off his neck.

A rap on the door broke into his desperate thinking. Without considering who it might be, he rose, unlocked the door, and opened it. A worried Morgan stood there, the gunman a step behind him. Morgan said: "This gentleman insists on seeing you, but I knew you locked your door and didn't want to be disturbed."

Panic sent a series of chills down Thorn's back. He had to fight an impulse to bang the door shut and lock it again, but he knew at once it would only make everything worse. The gunman would smash the door down and maybe kill him. Whatever the man did to him, he knew there was no way he could avoid this meeting.

"It's all right, Morgan." He nodded at Brown. "Come in."

Thorn backed into his office. Brown stepped into the room, and Thorn closed the door behind him. He walked to his desk and sat down, his heart pounding. He wished he'd left his gun on top of the desk. If he killed the man, everyone would certainly believe him when he said the fellow was trying to hold up the bank.

Brown didn't sit down when Thorn motioned to the chair across the desk. He shook his head and said in an even tone that was not at all threatening: "My name is John Brown. Cathy Allen and I will be married in a few days. I understand she learned something about you that you valued enough to offer her five thousand dollars to remain silent. You made that bargain with her, and now you tell her you are not keeping your bargain. Am I correct?"

Thorn nodded, thinking that maybe John Brown was not as formidable as his two guns were supposed to indicate. He said: "After I talked to her, I discovered that I did not have the funds . . ."

"You will find the money," Brown said in that same even tone. "I hate men who break their word, especially when they break their word to the woman I'm going to marry. It isn't just a question of my hating you. I'll kill you."

Thorn leaned back in his chair and stared at the grim face of the tall man who stood a few feet from him, his head tipped down so that his dark eyes seemed to be probing into Thorn's guts. In those few seconds he realized that Brown was fully as formidable as the two guns he wore indicated.

"I'll find the money," he whispered. "I'll have to take it out of my safe tonight after my cashier has gone home. I'll have it for Miss Allen in the morning when the bank opens."

Brown didn't move. His eyes didn't even appear to blink. After what seemed an eternity, he said: "She'll be here." He started to turn toward the door, then added: "I'm guessing you have a gun in your desk. If you make a move to get it, you are a dead man." Once more he started to turn, then paused again, his eyes still pinned on Thorn. "You hired a man to kill me. I ain't gonna forget that."

This time Brown did turn, reached the door in three long strides, and left the office. Thorn didn't move for several seconds as he struggled to control his breathing. He had an excruciating pain in his chest, and for a moment he thought he was having a heart attack. It passed, his breathing returned to normal, and he rose and left his office.

"You can go home, Morgan," Thorn said. "I'll close up."

"Thank you, sir," Morgan said. "I guess it is about closing time."

Thorn nodded and returned to his office. He felt there was something strange in the way Morgan looked at him, something strange in the tone of his voice. But it must be his imagination. Morgan was not a very smart man, certainly not an observant one, much less an imaginative one. Most people were stupid, Thorn told himself, and Morgan was more stupid than most. He had never asked for a raise as long as he had worked in the bank; he had taken Thorn's bullying without a word of protest. Thorn held him in contempt, and now he dismissed the thought that Morgan was any threat to him.

A short time later he heard Morgan go out through the front door and close it behind him. Thorn waited until he was sure that Morgan was at least a block away, then he rose, looked at the street door, checked the safe to see that it was locked, and returned to his office.

He put on his hat, not looking in the direction of the closet and trying not to think of what was in it. He left the bank through the back door, something he had never done before since arriving in Nugget City. If

Brown was watching, he didn't want the man to know he was not taking time to count out the $5,000.

As he walked along the alley toward his house, he felt immeasurably better. He knew exactly what he had to do.

CHAPTER
TWENTY-THREE

Ed made his rounds of the town much earlier than usual, the dusk light slowly blackening into night. He didn't expect to find anything out of line, but he needed time to think about Curly Wilson and what he might do. By the time darkness was complete, he had reached the business block and still with no more idea of what to expect from Wilson than when he had started, but he felt sure of one thing. Wilson would make a move soon, probably tomorrow. A grim thought came to Ed then. With Pete Egan coming to town tomorrow morning, Ed might not be alive when Wilson made his move.

He stepped into the Silver Star Saloon, not wanting a drink as much as he had a dread of going home. Judy might not have gone to sleep. Perhaps she had come back downstairs, and he didn't want to see her right now.

This was the first time he had ever felt that way about Judy. He simply did not know how to deal with her, what to say to her. As long as she felt the way she did, Curly Wilson stood between them, a prospect he could not face.

The saloon was almost empty. Three cowboys were playing cards at a table in the back of the long room. Lobo Wells was behind the bar. One man was standing across the mahogany from him, right foot on the brass rail, his head down so Ed could not see his face. A full glass was in front of him, but he wasn't drinking. He kept turning the glass with his fingertips, so preoccupied that he wasn't aware of Ed's presence when he stopped beside him.

Ed nodded, then saw the man was the bank cashier, Morgan. He had never seen Morgan in the saloon before. The cashier was not a drinking man, at least not in public. He had come to Nugget City three years ago, and Sam Thorn had given him a job. Ed didn't know whether Thorn had investigated Morgan's past, or even if the man had any recommendations from previous jobs, or why he had come to Nugget City in the first place.

Morgan was something of a mystery. He lived by himself in a small house on a back street and cooked his own meals. Ed had never seen him in the hotel dining room or the Bon Ton restaurant. He attended church but always sat in the back seat and was the first one out of the building when the service was over, shaking hands with the preacher and hurrying away, acting as if he was afraid someone would want to talk to him.

The townspeople considered him a queer one but regarded him casually because he worked in the bank. He was always courteous, tried very hard to please Thorn, and, as long as the banker was satisfied, no one criticized Morgan but accepted him in the limited way he seemed to want.

Tonight Ed had a different feeling about the man. It was so unusual for him to be here that Ed sensed something was wrong. There were other things that bothered Ed — the way Morgan stood, the tension that obviously was gripping him, and the fact that he had ordered a drink he hadn't touched — all intangible things perhaps but very real as Ed stood, studying the motionless cashier.

When Ed glanced at Wells, the bartender spread his hands as he nodded at Morgan, indicating he didn't know what was wrong. Ed jerked his head toward the other end of the bar, and Wells moved away.

"I don't want to be nosey, Morgan," Ed said, "but, if something's wrong, maybe I can help."

Morgan's head jerked up, and he turned to stare at Ed. "I didn't know you were there, Sheriff. What did you say?"

"I said, I didn't want to be nosey, but, if there is anything I can do for you, let me know."

Morgan was such an unknown personality that Ed would not have been surprised if the cashier had said it was none of his business, but he didn't say or do anything for a moment, then he nodded. "As a matter of fact, Sheriff, maybe you can." Morgan peered around to see that no one was close enough to hear what he said, but still he spoke in such a low tone that Ed had trouble hearing him. "I have a difficult problem. It's not as if I knew a law was being broken. It's just strange, not normal, you understand."

"Tell me about it," Ed said.

Morgan drew in a long breath. "I hope you will not mention this to anyone. I've worked very hard to please Mister Thorn. I don't want to hurt him. He gave me a job when I needed one, and I'm grateful. Naturally I don't want to lose my job. It's just that . . . well, by God, it's strange, that's all." Morgan swallowed, took in another breath, and blurted: "You see, Sally York came into the bank this afternoon to see Mister Thorn. She never did that before." He turned his head to look directly at Ed. "She never came out of his office."

Ed thought about that a moment, wondering why Morgan was so worked up about it. "Couldn't she have gone out through the back door? His office has a door that opens into the alley, doesn't it?"

"Why would she?"

"That is an interesting question," Ed admitted. "It isn't likely that she would."

"That's what I thought," Morgan said.

"You stayed late?"

"Yes," Morgan answered. "I left a little before six. Mister Thorn said for me to go home and he would lock up. There's nothing strange about that. He likes to stay in the bank. I believe he has trouble getting along with his wife. I guess he is more comfortable in the bank than he is at home. He often comes back at night, too. Not that he complains about his wife, you understand, but I have gathered from a few remarks he's made that he feels that way."

"I see," Ed said. "Well, what do you think happened to Sally?"

194

"I have no idea. All I know is that I never saw her again."

"Why don't we go to the bank and look around," Ed suggested. "I don't suppose this means anything, but I agree that it is peculiar. You probably don't know, but Sam has been acting very oddly the last day or so. You have a key to the bank, don't you?"

"Oh, I couldn't do that," Morgan said, as if he were shocked. "I'd have to have Mister Thorn's permission."

Ed thought of a few things he would have liked to have said, but he didn't say any of them. He understood how subservient Morgan was and what Thorn would be like as a boss. It was a wonder the man had said anything. He must have been very upset or he wouldn't have mentioned it. He studied Morgan a moment, sensing that Morgan knew more than he had said.

"I've got a hunch there's something else you've noticed," Ed said.

"Well, you see, I don't really know anything," Morgan said apologetically, "but it seemed strange that he was deeply interested in the gun fight between the stranger and Red Mike Kelso, and, when it was over, he went into his office and cried. It just wasn't like Mister Thorn. He's always so sure of himself."

"I'll tell you what I'll do," Ed said. "I'll go see if Sally's home."

"Fine," Morgan said in relief. "Well, I guess I'll get along."

He left the saloon in quick strides and disappeared through the batwings, leaving his untouched drink on

195

the bar. Wells moved back to where he had been standing, looking puzzled. "Now that," he said, "is a very odd thing. I never saw Morgan in here before, and I never saw a man buy a drink and go off and leave it that way."

"It's odd, all right," Ed said, and left the saloon.

As he walked towards Sally York's house, he wondered what Morgan really thought had happened. Apparently he had been relieved once he had told Ed, perhaps glad that he had put the responsibility on someone else's shoulders.

Ed found Sally York's house dark. He knocked, but no one answered. He tried the knob. The door was not locked, but that proved nothing as few people ever locked their doors. He pushed the door open and stepped inside. The room was black dark until he struck a match and, seeing a lamp on a stand in the middle of the room, lifted the chimney, touched the match flame to the wick, and replaced the chimney.

The room was immaculate, everything in its proper place. He picked the lamp up and went into the kitchen. Again everything was in its place, no dirty dishes, no food left out, even the top of the stove had been wiped clean of grease. He turned and crossed the living room to the one bedroom in the house and then stopped flatfooted.

Two large suitcases were on the floor beside the bed. He lifted one. It was heavy, obviously crammed with clothes. He looked in the closet. Empty! He pulled out the drawers of the dresser. Empty! He stood motionless for several minutes, looking around the room as questions prodded his mind.

Sally was packed to leave, but why? Why had she gone to the bank and stayed there? Why had she wanted to see Thorn? Certainly not to borrow money since she was leaving, and, if she had just intended to withdraw her money, she would not have needed to see Thorn.

Ed returned to the living room, set the lamp on the stand, and blew it out. He left the house, pulling the door shut and wishing he had a key to lock it. For a time he stood in the yard, staring at the dark house. All he could think of was to see Thorn in the morning. The banker had some explaining to do. Still, there was no evidence that Thorn had done anything wrong, and, if he said Sally left through the back door, there was no way to disprove it.

The town was very quiet, unusually so, it seemed to Ed as he walked home, the quiet before the storm. It would be shattered early tomorrow morning. He had hoped to find his house dark, but there was a light in the living room. When he opened the door, he saw that Judy was asleep on the couch.

She sat up and rubbed her eyes. "I'm glad you're back," she said.

"I'm sorry I woke you," he said. "I didn't know you were down here. I'd have gone on into my room if . . ."

"Oh, no," she said. "I wanted to see you. I couldn't wait till morning. I wouldn't have slept all night." She smiled ruefully. "I'm surprised at myself for going to sleep here."

"I wish you'd have locked the door," he said.

"The back door is locked," she said, "but your mother said you'd be in soon and to leave the front door unlocked." She rose and, going to him, put her arms around his neck and brought his face down to hers. She kissed him, a long and passionate kiss, then she said in a low tone: "I'm apologizing."

"For what?"

"For not listening to what you were trying to tell me at supper, and for walking out of the room. I should have stayed and talked about it, but it's like I told you. I had never thought about Curly's being anything more than a friend, but, when I got upstairs and lay down, I began remembering some things I had forgotten."

She turned away, suddenly upset. She walked to the front door, opened it, and stood staring into the night. "Like I told you, he was the one person who did things for me before I went away to high school. When I came home in the summers, too. At least up to the time you and I were engaged.

"What I remember most is that he liked to touch me, though at the time it seemed perfectly natural. On the arms, the shoulders, the head. He'd even pat my behind. Sometimes, when we were eating our lunch on Sunday after we'd fished a while, he'd reach out and take my hand. Then we'd talk about how it would be to be rich, how he could run the M Bar better than Pa if he was foreman. After Pa lost his leg, I didn't go fishing with him and I didn't see Curly except the same as the rest of the crew, but I do remember that he was always watching me when he was around."

She turned and faced him. "When I look back on it, after what you said, maybe all that touching wasn't as innocent as I had thought. And something else. I'm not sure, if he does want to marry me, it's because he loves me. I think it's because he'd get the M Bar. It makes sense now. He is a different man than the Curly Wilson I used to fish with."

She went to Ed and put her hands on his shoulders. "Ed, I understand why you're worried about me. If you're right, I've got reason to worry, too. I realize Curly is a very determined man. He's stubborn, too. At times unreasonably so. If you want me to go to the Abbots' place in the morning, I'll go."

"Good," he said. "I'd worry less about you if you were there. I know its illogical or improbable that Curly would try to take you back to the M Bar by force, but nothing around here seems very logical now. I have a job early in the morning, so it will be later before I can take you to the Abbot place. I won't be here for breakfast. I think I forgot to tell Ma."

She gripped his arms. "I don't like the sound of that. What kind of job?"

"Nothing that has anything to do with you or Curt or the M Bar," he said.

"I want to know anyhow," she insisted.

He hesitated, wishing he hadn't mentioned it, but she'd know sooner or later, so he said: "Pete Egan is bringing his crew through town and going on up to the M Bar. He aims to blow up your pa's dam. I told him I'd stop him right here in town. We can't risk letting him go on up the creek."

"Oh, my God." Judy turned away, then whirled back. "People are crazy. It's not just Pa. Egan will kill him and Curly and all the crew."

"There'll be some powder burned, all right," Ed said. "That's why I aim to stop him."

"He can circle the town," she said.

"He won't," Ed said. "Not after I told him I'd stop him. He'll give me a chance to prove I can."

"But you're one man against the Rafter E crew," she cried.

"John Brown said he'd give me a hand," Ed said.

"That gunman?" she said. "Why, he's as bad or worse than any of them."

"I figure he's worth about three men," Ed said. "I'd sure rather have him on my side than against me."

She stood motionless, staring at Ed, then she said slowly: "There must be some way of handling this. Maybe having Pa declared incompetent so I can take the M Bar over. I'll fire Curly and hire a new foreman. Egan would believe me if I told him he'll always have his water."

"I think he would," Ed agreed. "We'll see a lawyer about it."

"Well," she said reluctantly, "I guess I'd better go to bed."

She kissed him, then turned swiftly and ran up the stairs, the lamp at the head of the stairs throwing its thin light on the steps. He waited until he heard her door close, then shut and locked the front door, knowing that most or all of their problems would be solved by tomorrow night.

CHAPTER
TWENTY-FOUR

Sam Thorn did not want to make any explanations to Myra, so, when he arrived home and found her in her usual position on the couch, he thought he was going through the same actions he always did when he came home. He went into his bedroom, took off his hat and coat, and hung the coat in the closet, then returned to the living room.

Myra eyed him a moment, then asked: "What's wrong, Sam?"

His heart skipped a few beats. *How could she possibly know anything was wrong?* He sat down, after picking up the last Denver newspaper that had come in the mail. He said: "Nothing. I'm just tired."

She continued to stare at him, not satisfied with his answer. He held the paper in front of him, pretending to read, all the time cursing women for their second sight or whatever it was that enabled them to sense things they had not been told.

"I don't think you're just tired," Myra said. "I think that terrible gunman has scared you. Is he still there in front of the hotel?"

"I don't know," he said. "I didn't notice."

She said: *"Humpf,"* as if not knowing how he could possibly fail to notice.

"Well, damn it," he said, "I *am* tired. Pete Egan is behind in his interest again. I drove out to the Rafter E to talk to him. He's had money to build that fine house and furnish it fit for a queen, but he doesn't have the money to pay his interest."

That seemed to satisfy her, but all during the silent meal she continued to study him. He wasn't sure whether she had accepted what he'd said or not. He made himself eat. He wasn't hungry, and it was an effort to swallow each mouthful, but he knew that, if he didn't eat, Myra would be after him again.

He rose as soon as he finished supper. "I've got to get back to the bank. I need to go over some figures. If Egan savvies how things are, maybe he'll pay up. The bank needs the money."

"You go see young McCoy about that gunman," Myra said nervously. "If old Fist was here . . ."

"I know, I know," Thorn said impatiently. "I wish to hell Fist was alive and on the job."

He left the house a moment later and entered the bank through the back door. The dusk light was beginning to thicken, but it would be another hour or more before it was fully dark. He'd still have to wait a while after that to be sure no one was around.

He waited in his office because there was no other place to wait, each dragging minute moving a little more slowly than the one before. He was plagued by the memory of that horrible moment when he realized

202

he had strangled Sally to death, a memory so clear that he felt he was killing her again.

Sam Thorn had made mistakes before, mistakes that had haunted him for days and weeks after he had made them, but he had never made a mistake that was as terrible and irrevocable and foolish as this one. He wondered bleakly if he would ever be free of that memory.

He sat at his desk for a time, then rose and paced the floor, and finally went to the window and watched the last of the day die and night darken the vacant lot and the narrow slice of street that he could see. The town seemed deathly silent, without even the thud of a horse's hoofs in the dust or the sound of a voice. No one was moving along the board walk. The lighted windows of the Silver Star Saloon were the only sign of life that he could see.

He paced the floor again. He sat down at his desk. He returned to the window. It was all done without any sense of how much time had passed. At last he could stand it no longer. He opened the top desk drawer, took out his gun, slid it under his waist band, and then dropped a handful of shells into his pocket.

He tried to remember how big the moon was, or whether there was a moon at all. He had not paid any attention. Damn it, why didn't he notice things like that? Well, it was too late now. He had to move Sally's body, moon or no moon.

Thorn crossed the room to the closet slowly, steeling himself against what would be the hardest job he had ever faced. He opened the door, felt inside for the body, and found it, a shudder causing him to shake so violently he had trouble picking the woman up. He finally got her off the floor, staggered, and then managed to get the door closed. He slowly worked his way across the floor to the alley door, fumbled for the knob, found it, and pulled the door open.

When he stepped through the door into the alley, he found that there was no moon. There was even an overcast of light clouds that blotted out the faint starlight. Hell, he should have known there was no moon after staring through his office window. Well, he guessed, he was worse off than he had thought, and that meant he had to be very careful, but he was going to be all right. He knew he was.

Strengthened by these thoughts of self-assurance, he pulled the door shut and made his way along the alley, stumbling now and then over trash or a tin can or a stick of wood. A man was pounding on something in one of the barns, the lantern he was using making a faint blob of light on the dust of the alley. He hurried past, dodging the lighted area and hoping the man was too busy to hear anyone going past.

He crossed the side street, walking rapidly until he approached the rear of Sally's house. When he reached the porch, he stopped, panic paralyzing him for a moment when he suddenly became aware that someone was inside. Whoever it was must have been in the bedroom when Thorn was coming to the house but apparently had moved into the living room. There had been no trace of lamplight. Now there was.

For a few seconds he pressed against the kitchen door, frozen, wondering if the intruder would come on through the house to the back porch. He moved to a window and, looking through it, saw Ed McCoy standing in the center of the living room, looking around as if trying to see something that was invisible.

Breath was squeezed out of Thorn's lungs in an audible gasp, and for a moment he was afraid that McCoy had heard him. Apparently he hadn't because he turned, blew out the lamp, and left the house. Thorn couldn't see him leave, but he heard the front door being closed, so he assumed that he had. Obviously there was no reason for him to linger.

Quickly Thorn opened the back door, carried the body through the kitchen and dumped it on the living room floor, wheeled and ran out of the house, shutting the back door, and then stood with his back to it, panting, relief pouring through him in great welcome waves.

Luck was still with him. Then he began to wonder what McCoy was doing here. Whatever the reason, it boded no good for Sam Thorn. He had hoped that anyone finding the body would think Sally had broken her neck in a fall, but now McCoy, knowing that she wasn't in the house, would wonder where she had been. Well, Thorn told himself, he couldn't worry about that now.

He lost all track of time and didn't know how long he stood there, trying to make some sense out of something that didn't make sense. Finally he decided that one of Sally's neighbors must have come looking for her and, failing to find her, had gone to the sheriff. At least there was nothing to connect him with Sally's absence from her home or with her death. No one except Cathy Allen and the gunman, Brown, knew of his affair with Sally. There was no reason for them to spread the gossip now. For the first time it occurred to him that the $5,000 Cathy had demanded might be good insurance, but he didn't pursue the thought. He would go ahead with his plan. Remove Brown and there was no problem.

This last chore, he told himself, was one that would give him a great deal of pleasure. Slowly he made his way through the darkness to Cathy Allen's house. He had not really come to grips with how he would kill Brown. He'd had a vague idea of waiting until the gunman left Cathy's house, but now, standing in the alley, he realized that wasn't going to work.

He had been along the alley in the day time, so he knew where the porch and back door were. If Brown left the house through the front door, he'd be gone before Thorn knew he was leaving. On the other hand, if Thorn slipped around the house to wait in front, Brown might leave through the back door.

The more Thorn thought about it, the more he realized he was in a difficult position. Brown might even stay all night with the Allen woman, or at least until dawn, and Thorn knew he couldn't remain that long, even if he could endure the waiting. Too many people rose early in Nugget City, and somebody would be sure to walk along the alley and see him.

Too, there was a chance that Brown wasn't even in the house, but he immediately dismissed that possibility. Brown wouldn't stay in the hotel room when he could be here in the comfort of Cathy's house and be eating her cooking. Then Thorn considered going to the back door. Maybe Brown would answer his knock. If not, Thorn would push his way past Cathy and kill Brown.

No, he couldn't do that. Cathy would be a witness, and he couldn't bring himself to kill another woman, even as desperate as he was. Then he thought of tossing a rock against the back of the house, but Cathy would be the one who would probably come out to see what it was.

So he stood there in the alley, one wild notion after another running through his mind. From here he could see a shaft of light falling from a side window onto the yard, so they must be sitting in the kitchen. The blind had to be up, judging from the size of the patch of light.

Suddenly it occurred to Thorn that, by standing outside in the darkness, he could see the interior of the room, but anyone inside could not see him distinctly or perhaps not at all. The kitchens of the old houses in Nugget City were small, so if Brown was seated at the table, he wouldn't be more than ten feet from where Thorn stood outside the window. At that distance even a man who could shoot no better than he could would certainly hit his target.

Of course that was the answer. Why hadn't he thought of it before? He had been trying to find a difficult answer to a problem when an easy answer was right in front of him. Damn it, he thought bitterly, he had spent most of his life doing that very thing.

He lifted the gun from his waistband and moved as silently as he could to the rear of the house and then on to the side, stooping so that only his face would be opposite the window. He eased forward until he could see inside the kitchen. Brown was sitting at the table just as Thorn had guessed he would be, his side to the window. Cathy was carrying a coffee pot around the corner of the table, facing the window.

This was not exactly the way Thorn wanted it to be, but it would do. He cocked his gun, briefly alarmed when the click seemed as loud as a clap of thunder to his taut nerves, but neither Brown nor the girl noticed.

Thorn straightened, lined his gun on Brown, and fired. A second later Thorn realized he had missed. With the echo of the shot still hammering against his ears, he knew he was a dead man. Brown had dropped to the floor, yelling at Cathy to get down. He whirled, cat-like, and threw a shot at the window.

For just an instant Thorn was paralyzed, then he ran across the back yard to the alley and along it toward the bank. For some crazy reason he thought he would be safe if he could get there. He wasn't thinking now. He only wanted to get away, to hide, to lock the door of the bank where he could escape the whole chain of events that had happened to him since John Brown had arrived in Nugget City and had changed Sam Thorn's life.

He ran until he could not go another step. He heard Brown coming. He sucked in a long breath and staggered on until he reached the back of the bank and stopped again, leaning against the wall, panting hard.

For a moment he was unable to move, even though he heard Brown's pounding steps coming closer and closer. Somehow he found the strength to unlock and push the door open just as Brown's vague form materialized out of the darkness. He fired. It was a wild shot that missed Brown by three feet.

Thorn never fired again. Brown's bullet slammed him back through the door, and he was falling and falling until he crashed against the floor. He lay there, motionless, unable to breathe because his chest felt as if it had been caved in. Somehow he managed to say, as if seeking forgiveness: "I didn't aim to kill her."

Brown, leaning over him, barely caught the whispered words. He asked: "Who are you talking about?"

Sam Thorn did not answer.

CHAPTER
TWENTY-FIVE

Ed was sitting on the edge of his bed, pulling off his boots when he heard the shot. He straightened, head cocked for an instant, thinking the shot had come from a block away or more, then a second shot sounded hard on the heels of the first. He yanked his boot back on, grabbed his gun belt off the backrest of a chair where he had draped it, and buckled it on as he ran out of the house.

He sprinted toward the business block, having no idea what was happening. He expected trouble tomorrow with Pete Egan, and probably Curly Wilson after that, but he couldn't believe that either man had anything to do with what was going on here in Nugget City at this time of night.

Two more shoots blasted into the night just as he reached Main Street. They came from somewhere around the corner of the bank, he thought, and for the first time Sam Thorn popped into his mind. He raced across the vacant lot beside the bank, and, as he turned the corner, he almost ran into a man.

Instinctively Ed reached for his gun as he grabbed the man with his left hand. "Easy," a familiar voice said. "It's Brown."

Ed released his grip. "What the hell's going on?" he demanded.

"I just shot and killed Sam Thorn," Brown said. "He's in the back of the bank. Come on. I'll show you."

Ed followed the gunman to the rear door of the bank. Brown struck a match and held the flame close to the face of the dead man. It was Thorn, sprawled on the floor of his office just inside the door, a patch of blood spreading across his chest.

"I still don't know what happened," Ed said. "I heard two shots before these last ones."

Brown blew out the match and stepped back. "I was sitting at the table in Cathy's kitchen, drinking coffee. She was there, too, just around the corner of the table from me. All of a sudden somebody shoots through the window. I figgered he was after us, but the bullet came closer to Cathy than it did me. I got off one shot, but he high-tailed before I could pull the trigger again. I ran out through the back door, heard somebody going hellbent down the alley, so I chased him to right here. He took a shot at me and missed, then I drilled him." Brown was silent a moment, as if waiting for Ed to say something, and, when he didn't, Brown added: "Cathy will tell you what happened. I didn't have no time to coach her."

"I don't need to do that," Ed said. "I believe you. Sam's been acting queer ever since you hit town, paying Kelso to go after you and getting after me to run you out of town. What have you done to scare him like that?"

Brown was silent a moment, then he said slowly: "You couldn't jail a man for trying to do something that he never got done, could you?"

"No, reckon not," Ed answered, "and I can't shed many tears over Sam's getting plugged. He's been a genuine son of a bitch, as most folks will tell you, but he was never one to use a gun. You must have scared hell out of him."

"I ain't proud of this, Sheriff," Brown said slowly, "and, if you figger I've broken any laws, I won't give you no trouble when you throw me into the jug, providing you don't take it out on Cathy. You see, she got to prowling at night and found out that Thorn was sleeping with the school teacher.

"Cathy figgered we could blackmail him for some *dinero*, Thorn being the kind of man who wouldn't want that known around town, so she sent for me to back her play. He agreed to pay her five thousand dollars to keep her mouth shut, then decided he wouldn't do it. I paid him a visit this afternoon, telling him I'd clean his plow if he didn't keep his promise. He must have figured it was cheaper to kill me than pay Cathy."

"I'll be damned," Ed said. "So here was Sam, pretending to be a saint, and sleeping with Sally York all the time."

"One more thing, Sheriff," Brown said. "Just before he died, Thorn managed to say something about not aiming to kill her. I asked who he was talking about, but he died before he could answer."

"Probably Sally York," Ed said, knowing then why she had never left Thorn's office.

Men who had been aroused by the shooting began to cluster around Brown who stood just outside the door.

"Everybody stay out," Ed ordered. He stepped into Thorn's office, struck a match, and, finding a lamp on the desk, held the flame to the wick and replaced the chimney. Glancing around the room, he saw that there was no place where Thorn could have hidden Sally's body except in the closet. He turned to the door, saw Al Fleming and Buck Moore in the fringe of light, and said: "You boys lug Thorn's body over to the Cotter's place. The rest of you go home."

They hesitated, then Moore asked: "You holding this gunslick for beefing Sam?"

"No," Ed said. "It was self-defense."

"You taking his word for it?" Moore demanded.

"That I am," Ed said. "Now git moving. I want Sam's body out of here."

Still they stood there, eyeing Ed until Moore said: "You're the sheriff, but I ain't sure you know what you're doing. This here gunslinger shows up and scares folks to death, and now he plugs one of them. I say you oughta hold him till Judge Vance gets here for the next session of court."

"You can say what you damn' please," Ed said hotly, "but I am glad you remembered I'm the sheriff. I know what happened, and I tell you it was self-defense. Now I'll tell you something else. You've been raising the roof about Rafter E and the M Bar starting a shooting war here in town.

"Well, tomorrow morning Pete Egan is leading his men down Main Street. That'll put 'em right in front of your store, Buck, when the shooting starts, if M Bar should hit town at the same time. I told Pete I'd stop 'em, but me being one man and not having a deputy, it may be more'n I can handle. How about you giving me a hand, Buck? There won't be more'n nine or ten of 'em. With you standing in the street beside me, I think we can turn 'em back."

Moore stared at the ground, a boot toe scratching into the alley dust, then he said: "Al, get hold of his feet. We'd better do what the sheriff says."

Ed was silent until they had taken Thorn's body and the crowd had scattered, then he said: "Brave men, Brown. Looks like you'll be all the help I'm going to get."

"I figured it'd be that way," Brown said. "Well, I reckon we can do it."

Ed picked up the lamp, crossed the room to the closet door, and opened it, expecting to find Sally's body there, but the closet was empty.

Brown had stepped into the office. Seeing the expression on Ed's face, he said: "Figured she'd be there, Sheriff?"

"I sure did," Ed answered. "He's moved her, but hard to tell where we'll find her."

"Thorn was no fool," Brown said, "so he wouldn't leave her here, but what gets me is why he would kill her?"

214

"I don't know," Ed said thoughtfully, "unless he couldn't stand her leaving him. I was in her house this evening, and she was packed up ready to leave."

Brown nodded. "I'll bet that's it. They had a row, and he lost his temper. I can savvy that. No man wants to lose his woman."

"Sam was a man who always had to have his own way," Ed said. "Well, I'll see you in the morning."

"What time?"

"Hard to tell," Ed answered. "I'd guess they'll leave the Rafter E about sunup, which might put 'em in town between six and seven. I'll buy you breakfast if you want to meet me in the hotel dining room about six."

"You've got a deal," Brown said. "You sure you don't want to look at the window in Cathy's kitchen?"

"I'll take your word for it," Ed said.

He picked up the key to the back door that Thorn apparently had dropped as he had fallen, blew out the lamp, and locked the door. Brown had remained motionless in the alley, waiting, and now, as Ed turned to him, he said: "Sheriff, you're the first law officer who ever took my word for anything. I appreciate it."

"I can't see any reason for you to lie," Ed said. "Besides, I need you in the morning, and you can't help me in jail."

Brown laughed softly. "Sheriff, you are likewise an honest man to admit that, and I've met up with damned few honest sheriffs. I'll be on hand for breakfast."

The gunman walked away, disappearing into the darkness. Ed followed him to the corner of the bank building, then turned toward Main Street, wondering how much the law had to do with turning badmen bad.

CHAPTER
TWENTY-SIX

Ed slept fitfully and woke at dawn. He rose, shook the cobwebs out of his head, and went into the kitchen where he shaved by lamplight. He had finished when his mother, a robe over her nightgown, staggered into the kitchen, rubbing her eyes.

"It's still night," she said. "What are you up to?"

"I didn't want to wake you to say I wouldn't be here for breakfast," he said. "I've got an early meeting I can't miss. You go on back to bed."

She remained motionless, staring at him, still befogged by sleep. He put away his shaving gear and, going into his room, strapped his gun belt around his waist. His mother had gone into the living room where she waited for him. As he moved past her to the front door and passed to take his hat off the antler rack, she walked to him, her face reflecting the worry that gripped her.

"Where are you going?" she said. "I've got a right to know."

He settled his hat at the right angle and stood, looking down at her worried face, thinking how many times she had stood here at this hour, watching Fist leave the house for much the same reason he was leaving now. She had a nose for danger, he thought, after living so many years with his father. She should be allowed at this point in her life to live without worry, but maybe that point was never reached by a wife or a mother.

"You go back to bed," he said. "I've just got a date to have breakfast with a man in the hotel dining room."

He left the house quickly, knowing he hadn't fooled her, but unwilling to tell her he might never see her again. Fist McCoy had faced death many times, but he had died in bed, his wife beside him in her rocking chair. God willing, he thought, he would go the same way a long time from now, with Judy beside him.

He walked briskly to Main Street, the early morning air chill and penetrating as it always was even at this time of year. The light had deepened so that the mountain peaks on both sides of the valley were visible, the sun just beginning to show above the ridge line to the east.

When he stepped into the hotel lobby. John Brown was waiting for him. The gunman said: "You're a sleepy head, Sheriff. I've been waiting a good five minutes."

Ed grinned. "Sorry for the delay, but I'm glad to see you in such good spirits."

Brown laughed softly. "Oh, the prospect of a good fight is enough to brighten the whole day."

Ed led the way into the dining room and took a table near the street windows. He sat down as Brown dropped into the chair across from him. Ed asked: "What gets into a man like you who enjoys a fight, maybe even killing a man?"

Brown shook his head. "No, you're wrong about that, Sheriff. I enjoy a fight. I don't know why. Maybe it's the danger, or maybe proving I'm faster than the other man, or cutting a man down to size like Red Mike Kelso. But killing him?" He shook his head. "I hate killing anything. I don't even enjoy hunting, like most men do."

He was, Ed thought, a strange, complex man, and it struck him as interesting that he had learned to like John Brown. He had not been afraid of the gunman, as nearly everyone in town had been, and he had sensed that Brown was a prickly, withdrawn kind of man who had never really earned acceptance by others. Perhaps he had been persecuted by the law and had learned to protect himself by throwing out a shield of hostility. For some reason, which eluded Ed, Brown had been drawn to him, perhaps finding in him a sense of fair play he had not found in other lawmen.

"What kind of life are you and Cathy going to have?" Ed asked.

Al Fleming came out of the kitchen with a coffee pot, filled their cups, took their orders, then returned to the kitchen. Brown picked up his cup, stared at Ed as he sipped his coffee, then set the cup back in the saucer. For the first time since the gunman had come to Nugget City, Ed sensed a deep, soul-twisting kind of regret that comes to a man when he doesn't like the life he's living but feels he has gone too far to change.

"A hell of a life if we go on like this," Brown said grimly. "I ain't in no way good for her, but she loves me, and I love her, and I can't give her up. Not and go on living."

"Why don't you settle down here?" Ed asked. "I could probably find a riding job for you."

"I'd like that," Brown said. "I'm a good cowhand. Or was at one time. It's just that I've always thought a man was a fool to work for thirty a month and beans when he could make three times that with a gun."

"There won't be a demand for a man with a gun in Marion County once this ruckus is over," Ed said, "but there's always going to be work for a good cowhand."

"I know. The time for men like me is just about gone." Brown shook his head. "I dunno, Sheriff. I told Cathy this would be a good place to live. Out of the way where the men who want my scalp wouldn't be likely to think of looking for me, but she's had trouble with the women. Besides, I ain't sure how the people would cotton to me. I guess I'm still a threat to them whether I do anything or not."

They sat in silence until Fleming brought their breakfasts, Ed thinking of what lay ahead of them, of the likelihood that there was no need to worry about the future because there wouldn't be any future. When he considered how much his mother and Judy worried about him, he wondered how Cathy could face being married to a man who lived month after month facing the same kind of danger he was facing this morning and never being free from that worry.

Suddenly Brown said: "They're here, Sheriff. Right on time."

Ed rose. "Let's get out there and welcome them."

220

He stopped at the desk long enough to pay Fleming, then checked his gun, and saw Brown do the same. He admired the cold, efficient skill with which Brown handled his weapon, then he realized it was more than efficiency, almost as if the weapon were alive, more than a piece of iron that was a killing tool, but a part of him for which he felt a great affection.

"All right," Brown said. "We'll give them a fine welcome. You do the talking, but I'll speak my piece when it's time."

Ed nodded and stepped through the door to the board walk. There were six of them, Pete Egan and a grizzled old cowpuncher named Champ Albright in the lead. They had just passed the intersection of the side street that marked the edge of the business block when Ed stepped off the walk and held up a hand.

"That's far enough, Pete," Ed said. "I told you I'd turn you back. You go home and let the law keep your water flowing."

Egan pulled up and motioned for his men to spread out across the street. His red face was redder than usual. He had worked himself into a frenzy, Ed thought, and was hell-bent on seeing this through to the end. The danger was that his frenzy might control his thinking and push him past the point of reason.

Egan thumbed his sweat-stained Stetson to the back of his head and turned in his saddle so that his right hand was within inches of the butt of his gun. He said: "And I told you that we'd ride you down if you tried to stop us. I've got nothing against you, McCoy. Not personally. But I've lived with Maulden's threat to turn my water off for so long that every morning, when I get up, I expect to see the creek dry. I ain't going to go on living like that, so I'm going to put an end to it."

"No, you're not," Ed said. "I am, and I'll kill the first man who makes a move to ride me down. Now, you take your boys home, and I'll mosey up to the M Bar today and make 'em tear the dam out. The water is legally yours, and I'll see you get it. What you're fixing to do is just as illegal as what the M Bar figgers on doing."

Egan leaned forward in his saddle. He spoke slowly, firing each word at Ed as if it were a bullet. "Don't throw your life away, McCoy. Old Fist never backed away from doing his duty, but he always figured the odds."

"I'm getting goddamned tired of hearing what old Fist would have done," Ed said angrily. "Now, take your boys home before we start burning powder."

"There's six of us," Egan said. "You don't have a show."

"Two of us." Brown stepped off the board walk into the street to stand beside Ed. "That makes two against six, but the odds ain't quite that good in your favor. I can take three of you before you down me, and I'll start with you, Egan."

Ed didn't think Egan had seen Brown on the walk, or, if he had, he had not considered him a participant in his fight with Ed, and now, for the first time, the Rafter E man seemed to hesitate, his eyes flashing from Brown to Ed and back to Brown.

Throwing a quick, sideways glance at Brown, Ed saw that he had stopped five feet away, a lean, dark man who looked as formidable as an angry god. His feet were set solidly in the dust, both hands poised over the butts of his guns, and in that second Ed was convinced that Brown could do exactly what he had said he could.

"That son of a bitch will do it, Pete," Albright said. "Let's give McCoy a chance to do what he says he will."

The men at both ends of the line were backing their horses up and turning them to show Brown they were not in the fight. Egan apparently knew then that he had lost, that his crew wanted no part of this.

"We'll see, McCoy," Egan said hoarsely. "We'll see whether you're all wind or not."

He swung his horse and galloped north toward the Rafter E, Albright beside him, the others falling in behind. Ed watched, realizing only then that the sweat was rolling down his face, although the sun, still low in the east, had not warmed the mountain air.

"You're a cool one, Brown," Ed said. "I was afraid for a minute we had bitten off more than we could chew. I couldn't have done it without you. They'd have gunned me down." He hesitated, then he asked: "You think you really could have got three of 'em?"

The small grin that had now become familiar to Ed slowly curled across Brown's face. He said: "Son, never make a brag you don't think you can make stick." He turned toward the hotel. "I'm gonna get me another cup of coffee." He stopped, then nodded in the direction of the M Bar. "Looks like you've got more company."

Ed wheeled. Slim Parker, an M Bar cowhand who had worked for Curt Maulden from the time he had first arrived in the valley with his herd, was riding into town, leading a horse with a man's body lashed face down across the saddle.

Ed ran towards him, sensing what had happened, but not wanting to believe it. When he reached Parker, the M Bar cowboy said: "You can't change anything by hurrying, Ed. Curt's dead. Curly shot and killed him last night."

"How did it happen?" Ed asked.

"No way of knowing just what brought it on," Parker answered. "It was right after supper, about dusk. We were hunkered down at the corral, talking and smiling like we usually do before we go to bed. Curt was sitting in his rocking chair on the porch like he usually does. Curly . . . he got up and said he had to talk to Curt. It was too far away to hear what they said or see exactly what happened, but all of a sudden Curt yelled: 'You goddamned thieving bastard.' Curly drew and shot him."

"Curt didn't say anything after that?" Ed asked.

"Hell, no," Parker answered. "Curly wasn't more'n five feet away. He got Curt right through the brisket. When we got over there, Curt's rifle was on the floor beside him. He always had it with him when he sat in his rocking chair. Curly claimed Curt pointed the Winchester at him and was gonna kill him, so he shot in self-defense."

224

"You didn't see Curt make a move?"

"Hell, no," Parker said. "It was murder, Ed. Plain out murder. Way before daylight this morning Curly rolled me out of bed, told me I was fired, and for me to saddle up and take Curt's body to town. I was the only old hand left on the M Bar, you know. The rest of 'em are Curly's men. He fired all the other old hands, but Curt wouldn't let him fire me. Well, this morning Curly told me to get out of the country, or they'd kill me."

"Don't do that," Ed said. "You take the body to Doc Cotter's place, then you go to the hotel and stay inside."

He started to wheel away, but Parker grabbed him by the arm. "What are you fixing to do?"

"I'm going to bring Curly in," Ed said.

"Then take a posse," Parker said. "This ain't no one-man job. The others will swear Curly shot in self-defense. They figger on you coming alone, and they aim to kill you. Curly told me to leave the gate open so you wouldn't have no trouble riding up to the house. They figger on Judy's showing up there, too." He shook his head. "I'm telling you, Ed. I don't know what will happen to her if she does go. Anyhow, Curly wants the M Bar, and he thinks he can sweat Judy into marrying him with you out of the way. If she won't . . ."

His voice trailed off as if he didn't want to think of what would happen then. Ed told him: "You stay under cover, Slim. You hear me?"

"I hear you, Ed," Parker answered. "I know what you're thinking. If it should come to a trial, they won't want me testifying."

Ed wheeled away and started to stride along the street in the direction of his house. He didn't realize that Brown had come up behind him and had heard what Parker had said until Brown fell into step with him, saying: "I'm going up there with you."

Ed stopped and stared at the gunman. "This ain't your fight. You've saved my hide once today. Why do you want to do it again?"

The small, humorless grin was on the gunman's mouth again. "You owe me now. If you owe me enough, I figure you'll do me a favor . . . when and if I ask it."

"My God, man, I'll do it now," Ed said. "What is it you want me to do?"

"I'll tell you later," Brown said. "Right now I need a horse."

"Go to the livery stable and get one," Ed said. "Charge it to me."

Brown nodded, and swung around toward the stable. As Ed half ran toward the corner, he saw that Al Fleming was standing in front of the hotel, Lobo Wells outside the batwings of his saloon, and Buck Moore in the doorway of his store. They had been watching, Ed told himself, and not one had offered to help. Only a stranger who owed him or the county nothing had stood beside him when he'd faced Pete Egan and the Rafter E crew. As he turned the corner toward his house, a wave of bitterness swept over him. The people of Marion County did not deserve a sheriff who would risk his life to keep the peace, and for the first time, since he had pinned on the star, the thought of resigning was an attractive possibility.

He found his mother sitting beside the kitchen table, still wearing her robe, her uncombed hair still streaming down her back. He asked: "Judy in bed?"

Mrs McCoy nodded. "What happened?"

He told her briefly, then said: "Curly Wilson shot and killed Curt last night. I'm going out now to bring him in. Tell Judy about Curt when she wakes up. The body'll be over at Doc Cotter's place if she wants to see it."

He ran out through the back door, not stopping to argue with his mother when she called that he couldn't go alone. He saddled his horse, met Brown in front of the livery stable, and headed up the valley toward the M Bar, the gunman riding beside him.

CHAPTER
TWENTY-SEVEN

They had circled the M Bar and were hunkered down in a grove of aspens, looking at the ranch buildings below them. Ed had guessed that Curly Wilson would expect him to come alone and ride through the gate. If he had, he did not doubt he would have been cut down before he was within fifty feet of the house. It had been a long, hard climb to reach this point, but he had talked it over with Brown before leaving the valley, and Brown had agreed it was the only chance of action that could succeed.

The sun was noon high. It had taken the entire morning to get here, and that, Brown said, was a point in their favor. Wilson probably expected Ed to come after him as soon as he learned about Curt Maulden's killing, and, when he hadn't, the Bar M men would become nervous.

"I don't know these men," Brown had said, "but I've been in more scrapes like this than I can remember, and I've learned that you've got a better chance if you can make the other gent jittery."

Ed had nodded, thinking that experience counted, and he'd had mighty little. He'd gained a good deal in the last two days, and he was still alive, but, as he looked back over these last two days, he realized he had been lucky.

Fist had loved a lawman's life and had chosen it rather than the prosaic life of a miner or rancher, and his wife had paid for it. Thinking about his future with Judy, Ed told himself he'd never run for sheriff again. If he had his druthers, he'd put the wedding off until his term was over, but he knew Judy would not welcome that.

"You like being sheriff?" Brown asked.

It was a strange question, coming at this time when Ed's thoughts were running in the same channel. He asked: "How come you're asking?"

"I told you before I wanted a favor from you," Brown answered. "Cathy told me you were fixing to marry the daughter of the man who got shot. That right?" Ed nodded, and Brown hurried on: "And you're arresting the foreman who shot him, so what I'm wondering is who's gonna run the outfit?"

"I've been asking myself that," Ed said. "Judy will fire the crew, so we've got to find new hands, but I don't know of anyone in the valley I'd trust with the job."

"All right," Brown said. "I've got the answer for you, if you ain't real stuck on the sheriff's job."

Ed shook his head. "I sort of inherited it because Pa had been sheriff for a long time, and there wasn't anybody else who'd take it. It ain't that I mind wearing the star, but I don't want to put Judy through the worry of being a sheriff's wife."

"Well, when we were riding up the valley," Brown said, "I kept thinking it was a damn' purty piece of country. I've still got some doubts about folks taking to me around here, and about Cathy getting along with the women, but I reckon we could make it, so why don't you turn the sheriff's job over to me, or make me your deputy, and you and your missus can move out here?"

The proposition staggered Ed. There were obviously some drawbacks, such as whether a man who had been a hired gunman could restrain himself enough to be a lawman, but, in the few hours that Ed had known Brown, he had learned to respect him. If he made Brown his deputy, he could retain or fire him as the situation warranted.

"I think it is a hell of a good idea," Ed said. "Some of our respected citizens would raise hell, but, after the kind of support Buck Moore and the others gave me, I can tell 'em all to go to hell. I know one thing. Buck or nobody else wants the star."

He sat motionless for a time, as he turned the offer over in his mind, then added: "You know, I wanted to be a rancher more than I ever wanted to be a lawman, but the idea of cowboying for Curt Maulden or Pete Egan never looked like any kind of life."

They heard the clang of the dinner bell and saw the M Bar men begin streaming from the corral toward the cook shack. Brown said: "This is our chance, Sheriff."

Below them the aspens thinned out, but still farther down the slope, Ed knew, there was an irrigation ditch that Maulden had dug years ago when he had planned to raise his own hay. He had found it was cheaper to buy hay from the farmers in the valley than to try to raise it, so the bench had gone back to grass and the irrigation ditch had grown over with weeds, but that ditch would give them cover until they could reach the buildings.

Brown had been studying the layout below them. Suddenly he pointed to a shed that was less than fifty feet from the cook shack. He said: "If we can get to the log shed yonder, we'll have 'em like sitting ducks when they come out of the cook shack."

"No shooting if we can help it," Ed said sharply.

The tight smile tugged at Brown's lips. He said: "You've got some things to learn about handling an outfit like them boys yonder. You've got about the same chance of taking your man in alive as Curt Maulden had going for his rifle."

"Just don't get too trigger happy," Ed warned Brown. "That's the only doubt I've got about you being a good lawman."

"The one thing I'm not is trigger happy," Brown said irritably. "I've learned a few things about that, too. Always bluff your way out of a tight if you can. It's healthier that way, but Wilson ain't going to town to hang. He'll die right here before he'll do that."

"We'll see," Ed said. "Now let's move."

They ran through the scattered aspens, Ed leading, Brown three steps behind. They raced on across the open area beyond the trees to the irrigation ditch and dropped into it, panting. They lay there for several minutes, recovering their wind, before Ed began to crawl along the ditch. It was slow going, and Ed worried that they were taking too long, but, when they reached the closest point to the shed, Ed raised his head enough to see most of the area in front of the buildings. No one was in sight.

"All clear far as I can see," Ed said.

They crawled out of the ditch and sprinted toward the log shed. This was the make-or-break moment. If the alarm wasn't raised now, Ed sensed that Brown had been right in saying they'd have the M Bar crew like sitting ducks. Again they were lucky and made it to the shed unnoticed. Ed leaned against the log wall, breathing hard, more in relief than in need for breath.

He began to ease around the corner of the shed, but Brown caught his arm. "Wait till you've got your wind back," he said in a low tone. "You can't hit anything when you're puffing like a steam engine."

Ed grinned. "You're right," he said, and remained motionless.

"Ever kill a man?" Brown asked. "Or shoot at a man to kill him?" Ed shook his head, and Brown went on. "It's different from shooting at a tin can. Aim for his body and don't hurry your action. It usually ain't the first shot that kills a man."

Ed nodded, and this time, as he eased around the corner of the shed, Brown didn't stop him. An M Bar man was standing in front of the cook shack, staring at the gate through which he expected Ed to ride. As Ed stood motionless, watching. Curly Wilson came out of the house.

"Nothing in sight?" Wilson asked.

"Not a damn' thing," the man answered. "Maybe he ain't coming."

"You don't know Ed McCoy," Wilson said. "He'll come. He might be trying to raise a posse. You go in and eat, Monte. I'll watch."

They waited, each second an eternity, then the men in the cook shack began drifting outside. Brown nudged Ed with an elbow. "Time to take 'em," he said.

They moved toward the cook shack, Ed calling: "Curly, you're under arrest for the murder of Curt Maulden."

The M Bar men had been watching the gate below them. Now they wheeled, shocked into immobility for a moment. For a few seconds Ed wasn't sure what Wilson was going to do. The man in the cook shack ran outside, saw what was happening, and whirled to go back inside. Brown threw a shot at him that splintered the door casing.

"Stand pat, all of you," Brown said. "Not you, Wilson. You deserve a chance to make something out of this, but my advice is to shuck your gun belt and go in peaceful like."

Still Wilson didn't move, his eyes boring into Ed's, as if trying to decide whether he could outdraw Ed. Then he shrugged. "You've got no charge against me, McCoy. The old man tried to kill me. What do you think I was gonna do, stand there and let him do it?"

"That's not the way I heard it," Ed said. "You'll have your day in court. Now, saddle up. We're going to town."

Still Wilson stood motionless, then he shrugged and turned toward the corral. "All right," he said. "Just see that I have a fair deal."

For a moment Ed thought this was going to be easier than he had expected, that Wilson had meant what he said. The M Bar ramrod walked toward the corral and had almost reached it when, without warning, he whirled, drawing his gun as he turned. Ed knew he had been taken in, that he was slow getting his gun out of leather, but Wilson made the mistake of firing his gun while he was still turning.

Wilson's bullet missed, burying itself in the log wall of the shed, and, before he could fire again, Ed's gun was leveled and bucking in his hand. Wilson had made his play and lost. Ed's slug caught him in the chest and hammered him back against the side of the corral. He pulled the trigger again, but life had gone out of him, and he was already sliding to the ground. He lay there, motionless, his head propped up by the bottom log of the corral.

Nobody moved until Brown said: "The rest of you drop your gun belts. No use of anybody else dying."

"I ain't holding any of you," Ed said. "It was Curly's game, so get on your horses and vamoose. Keep going till you're out of the county. Take Curly's body with you."

They obeyed eagerly. Curly Wilson was dead, and Ed McCoy was alive, and they acted as if they were glad to get out of trouble so easily. Ed watched them go, relieved that it had turned out this way. He had not been confident that he could outdraw Wilson if the man made a fight of it. Now, starting at the retreating men, he felt no regret for killing the M Bar ramrod. Murder had been coming too easy to Curly Wilson.

"That's twice you've sided me today," Ed told Brown. "I might have got Curly, but Egan's men would have shot me to pieces." He extended his hand. "How do you thank a man who's done as much for me as you have?"

The small, wintry grin touched Brown's lips again as he shook Ed's hand. "It ain't necessary, Sheriff. You don't know it, but you've done me as big a favor as I've done for you. I never met a man before I could trust or who trusted me. Well, you treated me fair. I ain't one to forget it."

"As for that favor you said you wanted," Ed said, "about being deputy and all, it strikes me as the best way to handle the situation. Judy's gonna need a foreman, and I can handle it. I'll turn my salary over to you each month, and you can live in Nugget City and keep order in the county. It ain't a fortune, but you and Cathy can live on it."

"Sure we can," Brown agreed, "but will the townspeople put up with it?"

"I don't know which one of 'em can talk against it," Ed said. "The first one who does will have to answer a question. Where were you when I needed help enforcing the law?"

"I guess that'll shut 'em up," Brown agreed. He nodded toward the gate. "That your girl coming?"

Judy had just ridden through the gate and was coming up the slope at a gallop. His mother must have

235

told her what he intended to do, Ed thought, and she had hurried up here to see what had happened.

"That's my girl all right," Ed said.

"I'll go fetch the horses," Brown said.

Ed ran to meet Judy, thinking that, if the man with the two guns had not been beside him today, he would have died hours ago.